THE BILLIONAIRE MATCHMAKER TEST

BILLIONAIRE ONLINE DATING SERVICE BOOK #5

ELLE JAMES

TWISTED PAGE INC

THE BILLIONAIRE MATCHMAKER TEST

BILLIONAIRE ONLINE DATING SERVICE BOOK #5

New York Times & *USA Today*
Bestselling Author

ELLE JAMES

Dedicated to my family. I love you all so very much. You are the foundation, support and inspiration that keeps me going when times are tough.
Elle James

AUTHOR'S NOTE

Enjoy other military books by Elle James

Billionaire Online Dating Service
The Billionaire Husband Test (#1)
The Billionaire Cinderella Test (#2)
The Billionaire Bride Test (#3)
The Billionaire Daddy Test (#4)
The Billionaire Matchmaker Test (#5)
The Billionaire Glitch Date (#6)
The Billionaire Perfect Date (#7)
The Billionaire Replacement Date (#8)
The Billionaire Wedding Date (#9)

Visit ellejames.com for more titles and release dates
For hot cowboys, visit her alter ego Myla Jackson at
mylajackson.com
and join Elle James's Newsletter at Newsletter

"WHO CALLED this meeting of the Billionaires Anonymous Club?" Taggert 'Tag' Bronson asked, as he sat across the table from four of his closest friends at the Ugly Stick Saloon, a pitcher of cold beer being passed around.

"We did," all four of his friends answered as one.

Tag blinked. "Okay. You gonna clue me in on why?"

Coop Johnson grinned. "We've all completed the next step in our life plans by finding the women of our dreams."

"That is, all except one," Gage Tate said, giving Tag a pointed look.

Moose Smithson jabbed a finger in Tag's direction. "You."

Sean O'Leary grinned. "It's your turn to give the Billionaire Online Dating Service a shot. It's time you found the woman of your dreams, settled down and had half a dozen children."

Tag held up his hands. "Whoa, there. I don't see any of you with half a dozen children."

"It's only a matter of time before one of our ladies gets pregnant," Coop said. "After our wedding this weekend, Emma and I are going to work on baby number one."

"As are Jane and I," Moose added.

"Jane's really going to quit the modeling business?" Tag asked. "She's so good. I'm sure they'd hate to see her go."

"She says she's making room for the younger models." Moose chuckled. "I think she just wants to stay home and cook. She's amazing in the kitchen." He lifted a big shoulder. "And in the bedroom. Did I mention she's almost got the hang of horseback riding?"

Sean laughed. "Is that horse's name Moose?"

Moose gave Sean a narrowed glance. "Keep it clean, dude."

Sean raised his hands. "Hey, you started it with the bedroom and the horseback riding. Enquiring minds want to know."

"When are you two gonna tie the knot?" Coop asked.

"Soon. Jane wants to be on horseback when we say our vows." Moose grimaced. "I just hope it's not a complete disaster." He shrugged. "Me? I'd take her to

Vegas, get married in an Elvis chapel and call it done. I know she's the one. I don't need all the hoopla to prove it."

"Me either," Coop said. "But it's their special day. Anything they want, they can have. As long as I get a ring on my Emma's finger."

"I would think Emma's four brothers would be giving you hell about now," Tag said.

"Not at all. They did when I first showed up to date Emma. Hell, after I helped them haul hay, they seemed to like me better than their sister. I think if Emma had dumped me, they would have made me an honorary brother." Coop winked. "Good thing Emma didn't dump me." He glanced at his watch and grinned. "T-minus three days. You guys are still coming, aren't you?"

"Wild horses couldn't keep us away," Gage said.

"Racehorses could," Sean said.

Coop threw a cardboard coaster at Sean. "The point is, we're here to talk Tag into doing what we've all done."

"That's right." Gage turned his attention to Tag. "It's your turn to step into the world of dating."

Tag shook his head. "I told you guys I was working on a special project."

"And what project would that be?" Moose asked.

"Sorry," Tag lifted his hands, "I can't tell you. It's top secret."

"That's bullshit," Sean said. "You're the one who conned all of us into testing Leslie's BODS."

Tag raised his eyebrows. "And it worked for you, didn't it?"

"Yes," Sean said. "It did. I might not ever have asked Ava out if not for BODS." He shook his head. "Leslie really needs to come up with a different acronym for her online dating system."

"Whatever the name is, the system works," Tag said. "Sean has Ava."

"And Mica," Coop reminded them. "He got a bonus daughter out of that deal."

"Yeah, I did, didn't I?" Sean grinned. "She's a pistol, that one. So much like her mother. I love them."

"Exactly," Tag said. "You're happy. Coop's happy with Emma."

"I'm happy with Fiona," Gage said. "She's the best thing that ever happened to me. I thanked her step-sisters for entering her name in the database. If they hadn't done that, I would never have met Fiona."

"And Moose matched with Jane." Tag crossed his arms over his chest. "I can't think of anything more satisfying than seeing my friends happy."

Coop's eyes narrowed, and he glared at Tag. "He's doing it again."

Tag gave Coop a crooked grin. "Doing what?"

"Don't give us that innocent look," Gage said. "I swear you could sell ice to an Eskimo."

"You're avoiding the reason we're all here." Sean lifted his beer. "Well, besides the great beer and music."

"We're here to make sure you take a little of the snake oil you've been dealing the rest of us," Coop said.

"I'm working on it. I promise."

"Working on it?" Sean frowned. "Have you entered your data into BODS?"

Tag winced. "Not exactly."

Moose smacked his empty beer mug on the table. "Then you're not working on it."

"I'm going to," Tag said. "I'm just waiting for the right time."

"You didn't give us that option," Gage said. "You had a friend who needed guinea pigs to beta test her software."

"Are you disappointed with the results?" Tag asked.

"Far from it," Coop said and turned to Gage. "He's doing it again."

"We'll give you one week," Sean said.

"One week?" Tag frowned. "One week, and then what?"

Moose poured another beer as he spoke, "If you haven't entered your data into the system, we'll enter it for you."

"You're kidding right?" Tag looked around at his so-called friends. "There's no telling what the system will come up with according to your input. I need to be the one to do that."

Coop crossed his arms over his chest. "You've got one week to get 'er done."

Tag glanced down at his watch. "Can't you give me a little more time?"

"Nope," Moose said.

"Coop's wedding is this weekend," Tag said. "We're going to be tied up with that."

"It takes less than an hour to format your data and snap a photo," Coop said.

"But I had a plan," Tag argued.

"Plan—you're kidding, right?" Sean shook his head. "Love happens. You can't plan it."

Oh, but he was already in love, and the plan had to do with getting the lady to fall in love with him. In this case, that took careful planning. He couldn't tell his friends. They wouldn't understand. "Okay, then. I'll get my data entered and start looking."

"What do you mean, start looking?" Moose said. "Hell, it only took one date for the rest of us."

"Yeah," Coop said. "Trust BODS."

Gage nodded. "It works."

Tag couldn't jump right into making his woman fall in love with him. He had to ease her into it. Hell, he'd have to date some poor girls to appease his buddies while he worked on his plan. Which meant playing the BODS system.

His phone vibrated in his pocket. He pulled it out

and smiled. The beginning of his strategy was just starting into motion. He glanced up at his friends. "I'll enter my data this week. In the meantime, I have to go."

"What?" Sean glared at him. "This is an official meeting of the Billionaires Anonymous Club. Nobody walks out on the rest of us. Especially while there's still beer in the pitcher."

"Sorry, but I have to help a friend with some software issues." He pushed back from his chair. "Besides, you guys'll finish off that beer in no time."

Coop stood and extended his hand. "You'll be at the wedding?"

Tag took his hand and pulled him into a hug. "I'll be there."

"Will you be bringing your plus one from your BODS selection?" Moose asked. He stood as well and hugged his friend.

"I promised to bring Leslie." Tag grinned. "She feels responsible for the match and wanted to see the happy occasion brought about by BODS."

"She needs to sign up in her own system," Moose said. "She's a great gal."

"She is," Tag said. "And yes, she does need to sign up in BODS." That was his plan. To get Leslie thinking about dating again. Then he'd find a way to show her he was the right man for her, even if he had to hack into BODS to do it.

. . .

"I CAN'T BELIEVE the site is down." Leslie Lamb paced back and forth across the office. "I've tried everything I could think of to get it back up. I've rebooted the server, rebooted the modem, reinstalled the software and nothing."

Ava Swan patted Leslie's arm. "Don't worry. I called Tag. He should be here in thirty minutes."

Leslie's eyes widened. "You called Tag?" She shook her head. "He can't keep bailing us out whenever I can't figure out the system. That's my job. I'm the software engineer."

"And he's better at the networking aspect of BODS. He helped set it up."

"I know. I know." Leslie waved an arm out to the side, her pulse pounding, a full-on panic attack building inside. "He has his own business, a billion-dollar corporation, that requires his attention."

Ava cocked an eyebrow. "He spends an awful lot of time here, helping you, for a man who has a billion-dollar corporation."

Leslie smiled. "Ever since Randy died, he's been there for me. I don't know how I could have come through all that without Tag. He, Randy and I were such close friends from the very beginning."

Ava tilted her head. "What do you mean?"

Leslie gave her assistant and friend a soft, sad smile. "Randy, Tag and I met at a cocktail party hosted by a mutual friend, Chance Montgomery. You might have heard of him...?"

"Wow." Ava blinked. "Chance Montgomery? The most eligible bachelor in the state of Texas?"

Leslie nodded. "Back then, he wasn't quite the building giant he is today. He was a rising star, as were Tag and Randy. They were just hitting their stride. Anyway, we shared a ride home in a taxi." She shrugged. "The rest was history."

Her assistant's brow twisted. "You became friends after sharing a ride?"

"I know. It sounds crazy. They saw me home and made sure I got into my apartment safely. Tag and Randy bonded as well. They became good friends and included me on all their outings, even when they went fishing out of Rockport." Leslie smiled, staring out the window at the Austin night skyline. "We had so many good times together."

"But you married Randy, not Tag," Ava raised her hands palms upward. "Why Randy over Tag?"

Leslie chuckled. "I have to admit, it was a tough decision. Actually, Randy asked me. Tag didn't. I was ready to get married, settle down and raise children. So was Randy. I don't think Tag was. He was still working his way to the top." Leslie walked around Ava's desk and stared down at the photos her assistant kept of her daughter Mica. "We wanted children." She hugged Ava's shoulders. "You don't know how lucky you are to have Mica. She's an amazing little girl."

Ava nodded. "I know I'm lucky. She's the center of

my universe. And now, she's the center of Sean's and my universe. I can't get over how much she loves him, and he loves her."

"Love me, love my child?" Leslie asked.

"Exactly," Ava said, her gaze going to the picture of Sean, her and Mica at the fair. Mica held a fluffy, stuffed unicorn in one arm with her other arm wrapped around Sean's neck as he held her up. Ava had never laughed so hard or smiled so much as she had that night. The happiness in the photo brought back all the good memories of that night. "I'm so very lucky BODS matched us." She sighed and looked up at Leslie. "You and I have been together for four years at the Good Grief Club. Three quarters of the members of our therapy group have moved on to new relationships. Even I have taken the step with Sean. And I have a daughter, which makes it all the more difficult."

Leslie lifted the picture of Mica and stared down at it. "We so wanted children…"

Ava touched her arm. "You can still have children. You're still young. You just have to get back into the dating scene, find someone to love and get on with living."

Setting the photo back on the desktop, Leslie drew in a deep breath and walked into her own office then stood in the window overlooking the city of Austin. "Why do I have to find a man? Randy and I knew what was going to happen. Just because he's gone doesn't mean we can't have that family we always planned on."

"Excuse me?" Ava came to stand beside Leslie, staring at her friend's reflection in the glass. "It might be blunt and insensitive of me, but there is no more 'we' in this scenario. Randy's gone. Now, there's you. Just you."

Leslie smiled sadly. "I know. What you don't understand is that Randy banked his sperm. He knew he was going to die. We didn't get pregnant while he was sick, but that doesn't mean I can't still have his child."

Already, Ava was shaking her head. "Leslie, Leslie, Leslie. You don't mean this."

Leslie continued in a rush, afraid if she didn't, she wouldn't get the words out and that, somehow, not speaking them would make her change her mind. "It's called in vitro fertilization. They take my eggs and his banked sperm and combine them in a laboratory dish until the sperm fertilizes the egg. They implant the embryo in my uterus and voila!" She covered her belly with her arms. "I'll be pregnant. Nine months later, I'll have a child." Tears welled in her eyes. "And the beautiful thing is that it'll be a part of Randy."

Ava wrapped her arms around Leslie. "Oh, sweetie. You need to think long and hard about this. It's not so easy going into a relationship when you're a package deal. I know. It's not every day you find a man who's willing to accept another man's child as his own."

A single tear slipped down Leslie's cheek. "But that's just it. I don't have to find another man. I'll have a child to love. That's all I need."

Ava shook her head. "You're wrong. Remember how wonderful it was to share your life, your adventures and your love with Randy?"

Leslie nodded. "I do. And I'll have another human to share with in our child."

Again, Ava shook her head. "You'll have a child to love, true. Eventually, that child will move out, and you'll be alone again. And while the child is little, you won't have an adult to share your life with. No one to confide in when you're having a bad day. No one to lift your spirits. You have to keep the game face on all the time when you're a single parent."

"For my baby, I could do that. And I'll have eighteen years to get used to the idea of being alone again," Leslie argued.

Ava sighed. "Okay, so it'll all be good for you. But what about your child? What if you have a boy? Who's going to teach him how to play ball? Who's going to take him fishing and wrestle with him on the floor."

Leslie frowned. "I can do all that."

Ava's eyebrows shot up. "You can't throw a baseball to save your life. I saw you try at the fair. You couldn't hit the broad side of a barn."

Leslie's frown deepened. "I'll practice."

"What about football? What if your son wants to play football? If you think throwing a baseball is hard, have you ever thrown a football?"

"No," Leslie admitted. "Again…I'll learn. Or better yet, maybe I can get Tag to stand in on those occasions."

Ava threw her hands in the air. "Tag has a life of his own. One day, he'll find a woman to love, and he won't have time to drop everything to come bail you out on your computer or your child." Ava took her hands. "You need to think about this long and hard."

Leslie's jaw hardened. "I have. I set up an appointment with a fertility specialist. I'm going for my consultation in three weeks."

Ava's brow dipped. "Leslie, sweetie, I think you're selling yourself short. Look at you. You have a successful matchmaking business. You preach the value of BODS to your clients. You made me give it a try to be able to sell it to others. Why don't you give your own system a shot? See if you can go about this having a baby in the usual way…with a man you love and who can help you raise that child. Parenting is hard. Even on the good days. It helps to have someone to share the burden as well as the happiness."

The ding of a bell sounded, indicating someone had entered the BODS office.

"Hello!" A deep, familiar voice called out.

"In Leslie's office," Ava called out.

Leslie's face heated, and she squeezed Ava's hands. "You're not going to say anything to Tag about my appointment, are you?" she whispered.

Ava stared at her friend. "Are you going to give your system a try?"

Leslie bit her lip.

"Oh, my God," Ava whispered harshly. "You built it, you sell it, but you don't believe in it."

Leslie shook her head, her gaze darting to the door. "Of course, I do."

Ava dropped Leslie's hands and crossed her arms over her chest. "Then put your money where your mouth is."

Tag walked into Leslie's office at that exact moment. His brow furrowed. "Who's putting her money where her mouth is?"

"Leslie is," Ava said. She narrowed her eyes at Leslie. "Isn't that right?"

Leslie's cheeks burned. "I didn't say that."

"To what are you referring to when you say she's putting her money where her mouth is?" He gave Leslie a crooked smile.

"This whole BODS thing." Ava flung out her arms. "She sells it to her clients, but she doesn't really believe in it."

Tag frowned. "Why are you saying she doesn't believe in it?"

Ava answered for her. "She won't try it for herself.

If she really believed it works, she'd trust it to find her a mate."

Tag's frown eased into a grin. "I got the same lecture from my friends tonight. Can you believe it?"

Leslie let out a shaky laugh. "You did?"

He nodded. "Coop, Gage, Moose and Sean all ganged up on me and gave me an ultimatum."

Leslie's brow wrinkled. "An ultimatum?"

"They gave me a week to get on it, or they'd enter all my data for me." He shook his head. "Can you imagine what they'd enter on my behalf?"

Leslie laughed. "I cringe just thinking about it. So, what are you going to do?"

He shrugged. "I guess I'm going to give it a go."

Leslie's chest tightened. She'd always known Tag would someday find someone to love. He was a great guy. Why he hadn't married already was beyond her. But the thought of him dating someone else… Well, it didn't sit right in her belly.

Ava clapped her hands. "I think that's a great idea."

"What's a great idea?" Leslie asked.

Ava looked from Tag to Leslie and back to Tag. "You and Leslie can enter your data at the same time and compare notes as you review your potential dates."

No. That was a terrible idea. Leslie started to shake her head.

"You know," Tag said, "I think that's a great idea.

I've been hesitant to do this on my own. Having someone to help me evaluate and choose would be better than doing it alone. Two heads are better than one." He grinned at Leslie. "Come on, Les. What do you say?"

"Don't call me Les." She pinched the bridge of her nose, trying to think of a way out of this horrible idea. "I don't know. None of my clients have had help in the vetting process, and they've all found someone perfect for them by letting the system choose for them."

"Yeah, but you and I are closer to the algorithms than most. It wouldn't hurt to have a second set of eyes on the candidates BODS chooses." Tag turned to Ava. "Am I right?"

Ava shrugged. "Sure. Anything to get my girl out on a date."

"I'm game." Tag cocked an eyebrow in Leslie's direction.

"I don't know if I'm ready," Leslie said, shaking inwardly.

Tag took her hands in his. "It's been four years since Randy passed. He died. You didn't. I heard him when he told you to move on and find someone to share your life with."

"He said that?" Ava asked.

Leslie stared up into Tag's eyes. "He did."

Ava flung her hands in the air. "Then what are you waiting for?"

Leslie sighed. "BODS is down. It's not like we can jump in there and do it now."

Tag squeezed her fingers gently. "Don't worry. I'll have it up and running in no time."

"And while you two are working on getting your worlds in order, I have a date with Sean and Mica, and I'm late." Ava left Leslie's office, grabbed her purse from her desk drawer and hurried toward the exit. "Don't do anything I wouldn't do," she called out and stopped in the doorway. "Strike that. Do something I wouldn't do. Life's an adventure. Live it!" And she was gone.

Leslie realized Tag still held her hands in his. She pulled hers free, heat climbing up her neck into her cheeks. Tag was her friend. Why was she suddenly shy around him?

"What exactly is BODS doing?" he asked, his eyebrows rising.

"Nothing. I can't get it to come up. I've had several calls already from some of my remote clients. They can't get in online." She moved to her desk. "I can't get in at all. It's pretty much dead in the water."

"Let me take a look at it," Tag said. "I bet I can get it up and running in fifteen minutes."

"If you do, I'll take you to dinner."

"You're on."

"And if you don't?" She fisted her hands on her hips.

He winked. "I'll take *you* to dinner."

"Deal." Leslie glanced at her watch. "It's seven-fifteen."

"I guess I'd better get on it." Tag nodded to her computer. "Log on and enter your password."

She did and stepped aside, brushing against him since he was standing so close. A rush of heat washed over her from the point their bodies connected. What was wrong with her?

"I'll just work at Ava's desk." Leslie beat a hasty retreat to the outer office. "Let me know if there's anything you need."

"Will do. Fourteen minutes and counting," he said and settled in at her desk, his fingers already flying across the keyboard.

Leslie was torn. On the one hand, she wanted him to get the BODS system up and running. On the other hand, that meant she'd have to enter her data and join the dating scene again.

Her insides quaked at the thought.

And the idea of Tag doing the same should have made her feel better in a misery-loves-company way.

But it didn't. Not at all.

CHAPTER 2

TAG FOUND the issue with the BODS system in less than a minute, because he'd installed the glitch and set it up on a timer to shut down when it did. The timing couldn't have been better. With his friends ganging up on him and issuing their ultimatum, the call from Leslie's assistant, Ava, had come exactly when he'd needed an excuse to get away.

Actually, everything couldn't have worked out better. Even Ava making the call had been better than Leslie doing it. Having Ava at the office when he got there helped goad Leslie into trying her own system, making Ava look pushy, not him.

He was gleefully aware of everything falling into place. Now, all he had to do was look busy for fifteen minutes, push the button that brought BODS back to life, take Leslie out to dinner and begin his campaign to win her over.

He'd waited four years for Leslie to work her way through the grieving process after the loss of her husband and Tag's friend, Randy. Tag had been in love with Leslie since they'd met at Chance Montgomery's cocktail party six years ago. Only he hadn't been at a place in his life to make the commitment she'd needed. Randy had been there and made his move before Tag could. Because he'd loved them both, he'd stepped back, allowing Randy and Leslie the happiness they both deserved, all the while kicking himself for not letting her know how he felt.

After Randy had been diagnosed with cancer, Tag had realized that fate had played the right hand. Randy had needed Leslie to see him through to the end. Tag had been there as well, but Randy had died in Leslie's arms. A life cut short by a horrible disease. How could Tag resent his friend for the time he'd had with Leslie? He couldn't...and he couldn't bring himself to move in on the widow as soon as Randy's body was laid to rest.

No, Tag had been there for Leslie as her friend. A close friend. For four years.

Now that Leslie's matchmaking business was up, running and successful, Tag hoped she'd remember that she still had a lot of good years left in her, and she deserved a little happiness in her life.

He hoped and prayed she'd find that happiness with him. Tag just had to show her the possibilities.

At exactly sixteen minutes from the moment

they'd started the clock, Tag hit the button to reboot the BODS system. The Billionaire Online Dating System came right up, working exactly as Leslie had programed. "It's up," he called out.

Leslie came in and stood behind him, her hands on the back of her chair. "Oh, thank God," she said and sagged against the chair. "I owe you, Tag. You've saved my butt more times than I care to count."

"You don't owe me anything," he said. "In fact," he glanced at his watch, "I owe you dinner. It's been sixteen minutes."

"One minute is no big deal. I'm still buying your dinner."

He stood, shaking his head. "No way. A deal is a deal."

"But I don't feel right about you buying dinner when I'm sure your time is worth so much more than a meal. And I took you away from your friends." She frowned. "Is it too late to rejoin them?"

Worst thought ever. "Way too late. I'm sure they're back home with their significant others by now. Which leaves me on my own for dinner." He tilted his head. "Are you trying to stand me up?"

Leslie laughed. "Not at all. I just don't want to take up too much of your time."

"Being with you is never taking up my time." He hugged her shoulders like a good friend would when he'd rather take her into his arms and kiss her until they ran out of air in their lungs. Hopefully, that would come with time. He had a plan, and he'd stick to it. "What are friends for, if not to have someone to eat dinner with?"

She nodded. "Right." Her frown returned. "I guess it is about time we both took BODS seriously for ourselves. When was the last time you had a date?"

Tag shrugged. "I don't know." He'd tried a couple of times. A shudder rippled through him. Those dates were disastrous. The primary problem was that the women weren't Leslie.

"You work too much. And then you spend too much time helping me." She clapped her hands together. "Well, that's all going to stop now."

"What do you mean?" He wasn't sure where she was going with this, and he wasn't happy about her train of thought.

"I mean, you and Ava were right. It's not a bad idea to have a second set of eyes on the candidates. It's been a long time since either one of us had a date. Screening could be a nightmare. I'll help you, and you can help me. Maybe we will come up with the perfect match for each other. Ready to test that theory now?"

Tag shook his head. "I'd rather wait until tomorrow. I'm starving. I'm sure you haven't had anything to eat since breakfast. Am I right?"

She reached into her desk for her purse. "I had a handful of almonds. Does that count?"

"Nope. You need real food."

"What do you consider real food?" she asked as they walked through the office.

"I have just the place in mind." He glanced at her gray suit and frowned. "Don't worry. I think they have bibs."

"Bibs?" Leslie's brow furrowed. "Where are you taking me?"

"Don't you worry. I know how to treat a lady. Since I'm treating, I get to choose." He took the keys from her hand, locked the door to the office and slid the keys into her purse. "Ready?"

"I think," she said, her brow twisting.

He held out his arm. "We probably should brush up on our dating skills. If we want to do this right, we have to know the rules."

"There are rules?" she asked as they headed for the elevator.

"Not anything written." He tilted his head. "Maybe we should co-author a book on the rules of dating. I'm sure there a lot of people out there just like us who haven't been out in a while and could use some guidance."

Leslie laughed as they rode the elevator down to the parking garage.

Tag liked it when she laughed. "You should laugh more often," he said. "Rule number one: your date should make you laugh."

Leslie grinned. "And not because he's dressed like clown."

When the elevator door opened, Tag led Leslie to his truck parked nearby. "Unless he's actually a clown for a rodeo. Those guys are truly badass. I have huge respect for rodeo clowns. They save lives."

Leslie nodded. "Good point. Laugh if he's dressed as a clown, and he works for a rodeo."

"Right. Work is work. An employed man is golden." He held the door and handed her up into the vehicle.

"Agreed," she said, a grin slipping across her face. "You always make me laugh."

"And I don't even need a clown suit to do it." He winked and closed the door.

Tag drove away from downtown Austin toward one of his favorite restaurants. Not a high-class, expensive place but one he knew she would love.

"Rudy's Barbeque?" Leslie shook her head smiling. "I haven't been to Rudy's for…I don't know how long it's been. Probably since you, Randy and I came to celebrate the purchase of our office building in downtown Austin."

"I remember how much you enjoyed the ribs," Tag said.

Leslie laughed. "I needed to be hosed down after eating."

Tag glanced at her suit. "Like I said, I think they have bibs."

"Bibs? I need coveralls." Despite the idea of drenching herself in barbecue sauce, Leslie quickly unbuckled her seatbelt. "I like the pepper flavor of their barbecue sauce better than any sweet ones."

"I like the pepper, too," Tag said. "Something we have in common."

Leslie cast a sad glance his way. "Randy liked the sweet sauces."

"Yes, he did." Another reason he'd brought Leslie to Rudy's. He wanted her to enjoy the meal and to note the differences between him and Randy.

"Let me get your door." Tag leaped out of the truck and rounded the front in time to help Leslie down.

"I can get down all by myself, you know," she insisted, pulling her arms out of her suit jacket.

"I know." He gripped her around her waist and helped her to the ground. God, she felt good in his arms. "Rule two: let your date open doors for you and help you out of his vehicle. If he doesn't, he's not good enough for you."

Leslie's hands rested on Tag's chest. "Good thing you know all the rules. Your dates are going to love you."

There was only one date he wanted loving him. And she was standing in front of him, close enough to kiss. As if his body had a mind of its own, it swayed forward.

Leslie's eyes widened just enough to remind him he was to take it slowly. She had to come to the realization that she loved him on her own.

Tag reached around her to adjust the jacket she'd removed to keep it from falling out of the truck. Then he straightened and stepped backward. "Ready for some good old-fashioned barbecue?"

She ran her tongue across her lips.

It was all Tag could do not to groan.

"I am," she whispered. "The hotter the better."

His pulse quickened. He took her hand and walked her into the diner where they stood in line to make their order and waited for the cooks to prepare and deliver their food wrapped in butcher paper. Because they'd ordered ribs, the clerk at the counter handed them two bibs to go with their meals, as well as foil-packaged wipes for cleanup afterward.

Leslie slid onto a bench and tied the bib around her neck. She pulled a hair clamp out of her purse and secured her hair back from her face.

"You would have made a good Boy Scout," Tag said. "Always prepared."

"I take my barbecue seriously." She winked, rolled up her sleeves and bit into her first rib. Leslie closed her eyes and moaned.

Tag's groin tightened. "Good?"

She opened her eyes and gave him a saucy smile. "Amazing. I didn't realize just how hungry I was."

With a grin, Tag dug into his ribs.

Thirty minutes later, their fingers and faces were covered in sauce.

Leslie ripped open one of the wipes and worked

on her hands and face. She still had a little bit on her nose.

"You missed a spot." Tag leaned close and dabbed at the spot. Again, he was close enough he could have tasted the barbecue on her lips.

Steady, man. You're in it for the long haul. Don't blow it now.

She smiled and reached out to dab at a spot on his cheek. "There. Now, we're presentable."

"I'm going to wash my hands in the bathroom, then I'll be ready to go," Tag said.

"Me, too," Leslie said. "The wipes can only do so much."

They went their separate ways at the bathrooms.

Tag entered, washed his hands and face and looked at himself in the mirror. "Take it easy. She's worth the wait."

When he left the bathroom, Leslie was already standing, waiting in the hallway.

A man in faded blue jeans, a blue chambray shirt and cowboy boots leaned his hand against the wall beside her head. "Hey, beautiful. What say you and I go dancin'?"

"Sorry," she said. "I've already got a date."

"He ain't much of a date, if he leaves you standing around." The man touched her cheek. "If you were my date, I wouldn't let you out of my sight for a second."

Anger bubbled up inside Tag. He forced back the

instinct to flatten the man, face first on the ground. Instead, he laid a hand on the man's shoulder. "Pardon me, sir, but you seem to be lost."

The man spun, his hands coming up in fists. "Butt out, dude. I'm not lost."

Tag could smell the beer on his breath. "Yeah, well, you're hitting on my date."

"You snooze, you lose, buddy." He turned back to Leslie. "You comin'?"

She shook her head. "No, thank you. I'm with him." Leslie tipped her head toward Tag.

Beer-breath snorted. "He's a loser."

Leslie's eyes narrowed. "He's not a loser. If anyone's a loser," she lifted her chin and stared down her nose at him, "you are, sir."

"Why you—" Beer-breath raised his hand to slap Leslie.

Tag grabbed the man's arm, twisted it behind his back and raised it up high enough to make it hurt.

"What the hell?" Beer-breath yelled. "Let go of me."

"I will," Tag leaned close to the man's ear then spoke in a low, warning tone, "just as soon as you apologize to the lady."

"Ain't got nothin' to—Eeoooww!" he yelled. "I'm sorry. I'm sorry."

"That's more like it." Tag dug his keys out of his pocket and handed them to Leslie. "If you don't mind, you can wait for me in the truck. I have a little cleanup work to do."

She frowned. "You won't hurt him too badly, will you?"

He smiled. "Don't worry. I won't hurt him...much."

Leslie moved toward the exit, while Tag marched Mr. Beer-breath toward the clerk behind the counter. "Could you call for a police escort to take this man home? I believe he's had a few too many."

The clerk's eyes rounded. "Yes, sir." The young woman placed the call.

"I had one beer," the man argued. "One lousy beer."

"Sure, you have."

"You got no reason to hold me. I got rights."

Tag's jaw hardened. "You lost those rights when you swung at my date."

"I wasn't gonna hit her."

Within a few minutes, two police officers entered the restaurant and took charge of Beer-breath.

"You want to press charges?" one of the officers asked.

"No," Leslie's voice came from behind. "Just make sure he gets home safely and doesn't hurt anyone in the process." She slipped her hand through the crook of Tag's elbow. "Can we leave now?"

Tag glanced toward the officers.

They nodded. "We have all the information.

Thank you. You might have saved this man's life and others on the road."

"Just glad he didn't hurt my girl." Tag squeezed Leslie's hand close to his body. "Ready?"

She nodded and let him lead her out to his truck and help her inside.

Once they were both settled, she turned to him. "Was that rule three?"

He started the engine. "Rule three?"

"Never hit on another person's date," she said.

Tag grinned. "I hate to call that a rule since it's so obvious, but you're right. It's not good to hit on another person's date. Don't do it."

Leslie buckled her seatbelt, draped her jacket over her lap and smiled at the windshield ahead of her. "It seems I have a lot to remember and learn. And thank you for taking over with that redneck back there. I could have taken care of myself, though."

Tag shot a glance in her direction. "He was about to hit you."

"I was about to duck and knee him in the crotch."

"In that skirt?" Tag raised a brow. "I don't think you could have gotten your knee up high enough."

"I would have raised it." She shook her head. "But thank you for saving me from that goon."

"You're welcome." He pulled out of the parking lot. "Where to? Want to go dancing?" He winked. "You might be disappointed you couldn't go with Beer-breath."

"Not tonight," Leslie said. "Though I do love to dance. Maybe another night." She brightened. "I'll put that down as one of my preferences. A man who likes to dance."

"Good idea. I'll put that down as well. I love to dance."

Leslie's brow scrunched. "You like to dance? I seem to remember you didn't."

"I'll have you know I took lessons. I learned a long time ago that most women love to dance. If I wanted to impress one, all I had to do was offer to take her dancing."

Leslie studied him. "When did you learn how to dance?"

"Several years ago. I took lessons in ballroom dancing. I can waltz, foxtrot, tango and samba. I also know a few line dances, and I can do a mean two-step."

Leslie frowned. "Taggert Bronson, do I even know you?"

Tag grinned, glad he'd finally gotten her attention. "Sometimes, I don't think you do."

"Well, that has to change." She folded her arms in her lap. "I'll know all about you after we work on your profile in BODS. We'll find you a perfect match. The ladies are going to love you."

Tag stared at the road ahead. That wasn't exactly what he'd had in mind when he'd gotten her attention. He wanted her to consider him as perfect for her, not some other woman.

He could see that he still had work to do.

LESLIE SAT in the seat next to Tag, wondering what the heck was wrong with her. Tag was her dearest friend. He'd been Randy's best friend. Why was she thinking about him as date material?

She tried to tell herself it was because she had to think of him as a client and determine what would appeal to her female clients.

However, it was more than that. She liked being with him. She'd always enjoyed being with him, even when she, Randy and Tag had been friends, before she'd agreed to marry Randy. Now, with Randy gone, she was thinking of Tag as more than a friend. A couple times this evening, she'd had the sudden and startling urge to kiss him.

Holy hell. Tag would have been appalled. She was married to his best friend!

Was.

Randy was gone. He wouldn't have minded if Leslie fell in love again. He'd even said he didn't want her to be alone. Randy had given her permission to fall in love and have a chance at happiness. How would he have felt if he'd known she was looking at Tag in that way?

Knowing Randy, he would have loved the idea of Tag taking care of her.

Leslie risked a glance at Tag from beneath her lashes.

He was every bit as handsome as Randy had been, maybe even more so. His blue eyes contrasted so well with his dark brown hair. He was taller than Randy, and his shoulders were broader.

"Have you been working out?" Leslie asked before she thought.

Tag's lips twitched. "I try to stay in shape," he admitted. "I have a home gym where I lift weights, and I go to the gym three times a week to spar with a retired boxer."

Leslie raised her eyebrows. "I'm impressed."

He shrugged. "Keeps me from getting bored."

"You? Bored?" Leslie shook her head. "As I remember, you never slowed down enough to get bored."

Tag snorted. "When I started making money, I had to hire other people to help manage my holdings. I did such a good job hiring people who could do the work, I don't have as much to do."

"Is that why you're always over messing with my little BODS system?"

He nodded. "Truth is, I'm never bored around you."

Leslie's heart swelled. "Same."

"If we're going to do this dating thing, I'll be seeing even more of you." He tipped his head toward her, raising his eyebrows.

"The idea is to see a lot more of your date," she reminded him.

"Right." He nodded. "But until I find the right woman for me and you find the right man for you, we're going to help each other sift through the candidates."

Leslie nodded. "That's the plan."

"What time do you want me at your office tomorrow?"

Leslie blinked. "I don't know. What time is good for you?"

"I could be there in the afternoon around four-thirty or five, if that's not too late."

"That would be perfect," she said, her voice a little breathy. The thought of entering her personal profile in front of Tag made her wonder if she was doing the right thing. Then again, he knew her. Probably better than she knew herself.

Leslie frowned. She'd thought she knew him. The fact that he'd taken dance lessons, and she didn't know that about him, made her question just how well she knew Taggert Bronson.

"Why have you never married?" she asked.

Tag laughed. "That was out of nowhere."

"Not really. It would help me to know this information if I'm going to help you find a perfect match."

Tag shrugged. "I guess I wasn't ready."

"Have you ever been in love?" After the words left

her mouth, her breath caught and held in her throat. She had to know.

He drew in a deep breath, his brow descending as if he was thinking about his answer. "I fell in love once."

She leaned toward him, her heartbeat ratcheting up. "And? What happened?"

He slowed for a streetlight, staring ahead through the window. "I wasn't ready. She was."

"And she married someone else?" Leslie's heart pinched in her chest. She reached out and touched his arm. "I'm sorry."

"Don't be." He patted her hand. "I think it was meant to be."

"Did she know you loved her?" Leslie asked.

He shook his head.

She frowned. "Did I know her?"

"Maybe," he said. "It doesn't matter. It was a long time ago."

Leslie sensed he didn't want to talk about it. It had to have been a painful loss for Tag to avoid marriage.

"Maybe she wasn't the right one for you," Leslie suggested.

"Oh, she was the right one. I was too immature to realize it until it was too late." He spoke with a hint of self-loathing that cut straight through to Leslie's heart.

"Wow." Leslie shook her head. "She must have been amazing."

"She is."

"It was her loss, as far as I'm concerned." Leslie squeezed his arm. "Don't worry. We'll find someone even better. A woman who won't miss what a great guy you are. You're going to make the best husband and father."

"Assuming she wants kids," he interjected.

"Do you want kids?" Leslie asked. Again, her breath caught and held. Not that Tag's stance on children had anything to do with her.

"Absolutely," Tag said. "I want four. Two boys and two girls. But I'd take all boys and all girls, as long as they're all healthy."

Leslie laughed. "That's how many I want. One is so lonely. Two is lovely, but I would adore having a houseful of noise and laughter."

He smiled in her direction. "You were an only child, right?"

She nodded. "I always wanted siblings to play with."

"I was number three of four children," Tag said.

"Your father was military, wasn't he?" Leslie asked.

Tag nodded. "We moved so many times while I was young, I don't know what I would have done without my brother and sisters. They were my friends when I didn't know anyone else." He smiled. "Life was always an adventure in our family."

"Can I tell you a secret?" Leslie bunched her

hands into fists. It might be a mistake, but she wanted him to know.

"Sure. Your secrets are always safe with me." He glanced her way, his brow furrowing. "You're all right, aren't you? No serious health issues, I hope?"

She laughed. "No. Nothing like that. I'm fine. I just…" Was it right to tell him before she even tried? "If things don't work out with BODS," she said, "I'm thinking of having a baby on my own."

Tag's foot stomped on the brake. "What?"

"Oh, dear." She pitched forward, grabbed the "oh-shit" handle by the door and righted herself. "I guess I shouldn't have said anything. Especially while you're driving."

"No. No. I'm glad you did. Something like having a baby is a big deal. Talking about it helps with the decision." He shook his head. "How will you do that without a father?"

She looked down at her hands. "When Randy found out he was terminal, I insisted he save his sperm. We always wanted children. We tried to get pregnant, but," she shrugged, "it never happened."

"Oh, sweetheart." He caught her hand and held it in his. "We both have regrets. But we can't keep looking back. We have to look forward. Just because things didn't turn out the way we thought it should doesn't mean it won't turn out the way it was supposed to be all along."

Leslie nodded. "You're right. Maybe I was

supposed to be a single mom, raising a child on my own." A tear slipped from the corner off her eye. She quickly wiped it away. "No matter what, we have to see this through. I made a promise to give BODS a try. If all else fails, I have a Plan B."

"Promise me you'll give dating a shot. You deserve to have all the happiness. That means someone to love, who loves you, and four rambunctious kids to raise the rooftop with noise."

Leslie chuckled, the sound catching a little. "You're right. I need to be open to the possibilities."

"You never know...the person you were meant to be with could be right there waiting for you. You have to keep your eyes open and recognize love for what it is."

She nodded. "You're right." Leslie smiled at him. "I don't know what I'd do without you, Tag. You're the best friend a girl could ever have."

His lips twisted. "Here we are," he said, pulling into the driveway of the home she and Randy had built together the year before he was diagnosed.

"Wow, we got here fast," she said, reaching for the buckle of her seatbelt.

Tag dropped down out of the pickup and hurried around to open her door for her.

Once again, he gripped her waist in his strong hands and lifted her down to the ground.

Now that she knew those muscles were real and he worked for them, she could appreciate how hard they were against her palms. Her heartbeat stuttered, and her insides heated.

Any woman would be excited this close to Tag. He was one hundred percent male, tough enough to take care of a redneck and gentle enough to hold doors for the ladies. Some lucky woman was going to be thrilled to be matched with Taggert Bronson.

Why she wasn't thrilled with that idea had her stumped.

Tag walked her to the door of her house and held out his hand for her keys. After he unlocked her door and opened it, he handed back the keys, his fingers holding onto the keyring a little longer than necessary.

His touch caused a rush of electricity to radiate from her fingers up her arm and throughout her body.

He stood so close she could feel the heat from his body against hers. If she leaned up on her toes, she could brush her lips across his. How would that feel?

Tag cupped her cheek in his palm and lowered his head.

Her gaze on his mouth, Leslie watched as he grew closer.

Instead of his mouth claiming hers, he altered course and lightly touched his lips to her forehead. "Goodnight, Leslie."

Then he stepped away, leaving her feeing like she'd missed something very important.

"Do you want to come in for a drink?" she blurted out.

"I'd like nothing better," he said. "But I actually have to go to a meeting first thing in the morning." He gave her a quick smile. "I'll see you tomorrow afternoon."

She nodded. "Tomorrow." Leslie entered her house, closed the door behind her and leaned against it. Had he almost kissed her? And if he had, would she have liked it as much as she thought she would?

CHAPTER 3

TAG ARRIVED fifteen minutes early at the BODS office building and sat in his truck, waiting for the exact time he said he'd be there. While he waited, he called Coop.

"Getting cold feet?" Coop asked without preamble.

"No way. I'm ready for this."

Coop snorted. "If you're so ready, why did you wait so long to give BODS a chance?"

"The timing wasn't right," Tag said. None of his buddies in the Billionaire Anonymous Club knew about his love for Leslie, and he preferred they remain clueless until his plan came together.

"Have you been going through your little black book, breaking the news to all of your former girl-friends?" Coop asked.

"Don't have one. Don't have any."

"Hmm. That's right. You have been single for a while. No wonder you're ready."

"I've been busy with work and the ranch. No time for relationships," he explained, knowing his answer was a bit simplistic.

"You had plenty of time to work with Leslie getting the rest of us involved in relationships. It's about time you worked on you." Coop paused. "Is Leslie going to help you like she helped us get set up?"

"That's the plan." Tag glanced at the clock. "I'm at her office building right now, about to go up and enter my data."

"And you called me for moral support?" Coop chuckled. "All I have to say is BODS worked for me. As far as I can tell, it worked for Gage, Sean and Moose, as well. You've got nothing to lose."

Oh, he had a lot to lose, if Leslie chose another man over him. Again.

"Look, Tag," Coop said. "The best thing you can do is to enter the truth about yourself. BODS will come up with your perfect match. Trust the system to get it right."

"Thanks, man. I'll let you know how it goes."

"Good. I'm anxious to meet the future Mrs. Bronson."

"Gotta go," Tag said. "Thanks for your support."

"Anytime."

Tag ended the call and slipped out of his truck at

exactly five minutes before he was due to show up in Leslie's office. The ride up the elevator was short with no stops along the way to delay his arrival.

"Good afternoon, Mr. Bronson," Ava greeted him as he stepped into the office.

Tag shook his head. "Ava, you know me. You don't have to be all formal."

She grinned. "I know. It's just that you're here to use the BODS system. You're a client now, not just a friend." She rounded the corner of her desk and gave him a hug. "Don't be apprehensive about this part of the journey. It's easy."

"That's right," Tag said. "You've done this before."

She nodded. "I have. If not for BODS, I might never have learned Sean was my perfect match. Not only my match as a date, but as a father to Mica." She smiled. "We couldn't be happier."

"I'm glad to hear that." He hugged her back. "Sean loves you and Mica. It's pretty obvious."

"And we love him." She waved a hand toward a hallway. "Leslie asked me to show you into the conference room where you two will be working to enter your profiles and start the process."

"Where's Leslie?"

"She's in her office, talking to a client. She'll be right with you." Ava opened a door and walked into the conference room where two computer monitors and keyboards were set up for their use. "I think I'm more excited about her giving her system a try than she is," Ava said.

"Is she nervous?"

Ava laughed. "Terribly."

"Why? She doesn't have to go out with anyone she doesn't want to."

"I know that, and she knows that, but it's been a long time since she's been on a date."

His lips twisting, Tag nodded. "Tell me about it."

Ava cocked an eyebrow. "You, too?"

"Yeah," Tag said. "I've been pretty busy with my work." Getting all the right people in the right place to manage his businesses and allow him the time he needed to woo the woman he loved.

"Let me get the application up." She started to take the seat behind the keyboard.

"No need," he said. "I'm pretty familiar with the system."

Ava laughed. "That's right. You helped Leslie get it up and running. Silly me." She held out the chair. "Then I'll leave you to it. I believe Leslie's already entered some of her data. She said something about helping you with yours."

"I'll get started, and she can help when she's ready. Thanks."

Ava left the room, closing the door behind her.

Tag sat in the seat in front of one of the monitors, clicked on the mouse and brought up the initial data entry screen.

What he hadn't told Leslie was that he'd entered data anonymously, bypassing her background checks. He'd also entered a blurred image that would make it impossible for her to know it was him.

The name he'd used was one he'd picked up from a romantic comedy his mother and sisters had forced him to watch with them when he was a kid—the movie, *You Got Mail*, about a man and a woman who met online and fell in love through their messages. He'd chosen the lead character's name, Joe Fox, as his alternate ego name on the BODS systems and manipulated the data to get around the background checks.

As soon as Leslie had all her data and preferences entered, Tag would match her preferences and start an online conversation with her while she was going through her dates. He liked the idea of her falling in love with the man behind the curtain. When the time came, he'd reveal himself as her online pen pal.

It all sounded like a good plan. He just hoped he had enough time to build the relationship before she found someone else through BODS matching algorithms.

Tag drew in a deep breath. No matter what happened, he hoped Leslie found love. She deserved to be happy. He prayed it would be with him.

To maintain a modicum of privacy, he entered his nickname into the system as Tag Bronson. The only people who called him Tag were his BAC friends, their ladies and Leslie. The media knew Taggert

Bronson as the Texas billionaire and one of the most eligible bachelors in the state. He didn't want any of his dates to be with groupies who were only after his money. He didn't want the press to create a media circus out of his experimental dating.

Once he had his primary data entered, he dove into his preferences.

Must love dogs.

Must like the outdoors.

Must like steak. No vegans, please.

Ability to ride horses preferred, not required. He could teach that.

"Must love ballroom dancing," a voice said behind him.

Tag looked up into Leslie's smiling face, and his heart flipped over several times. "I didn't hear you come in," he said.

"I'm stealthy like that," she said with a wink and took the seat beside him. "I started entering my preferences but got stuck. It appears I don't know myself as well as I'd like to think I do."

"I can help you with that," he said. "Bring yours up. While you wait for your profile to boot, you can help me with mine."

She clicked the mouse and entered her login and password. While she waited, she turned to his monitor. "Favorite color?" she asked. "Isn't it blue?"

Tag nodded. "And yours is yellow. You love sunshine."

She nodded. "I do so love sunshine."

"As much as you love sunshine," Tag said, "you enjoy walking in the rain, as long as you don't have to be anywhere that your hair matters."

Leslie laughed. "Right. And you love the rain because it means fresh grass for your horses."

"Speaking of horses, don't forget to mark that you ride. That might impress your prospects." He waved toward her monitor. "Your profile just came up."

"Good," she said and quickly scrolled to the preferences page. "Yellow for favorite color. Rides horses."

"Loves dancing," Tag reminded her.

"Favorite flower," Leslie paused.

"Bluebonnets," Tag said. "You love the bluebonnets in the spring."

"That's right." Leslie sat back, a smile curling her lips. "Remember the time we drove out to Enchanted Rock and almost didn't make it in time to hike to the top?"

"We stopped so many times for you to take pictures of the bluebonnets and Indian paintbrushes along the side of the road, it was late afternoon before we got to the base of Enchanted Rock."

"Randy almost called off our hike," Leslie said.

"I'm glad he didn't," Tag said. "The hike was great, and the view from the top was amazing."

Leslie stared at the monitor, her hands in her lap.

"Thankfully, we got down before it was too dark to navigate the boulders."

"I remember we were so hungry, we stopped at that little German café on the way back and had wiener schnitzel and beer."

"You and Randy drank too much beer, and I ended up driving us all home." Leslie glanced toward him. "That was the month before Randy was diagnosed." She sighed. "I'm glad we went. It made for good memories. We were all happy then."

Tag remembered. He hadn't been married to Leslie, but he'd still enjoyed her company, and he couldn't begrudge his best friend's happiness. Though he'd been a third wheel on the trip, he was still glad he'd gone. He'd loved Randy, too. As a brother.

"Must love cats," Leslie entered.

"Cats?" Tag shook his head. "Since when do you love cats?"

"I've always loved cats. Randy wouldn't let me have one in the house," Leslie said. "He said he was allergic. I think he just didn't like them."

Tag made a note to include cats as a preference for his alter ego. He didn't have a problem with cats, but he preferred dogs.

"What about dogs?"

"Must love dogs. But most men do," Leslie shook her head. "Unfortunately, cats can be a deal-breaker for some men. I want my man to be open to felines."

"Fair enough," Tag said. "I like cats, especially the ones that live in my barn and keep the mouse population down."

"See? That's what I love about you," she said. "You're open to the possibilities."

Whew, Tag thought. He'd dodged the cat bullet.

"Preferences in looks…" Leslie stared at the screen. "I really don't think looks matter all that much. It's what's on the inside that I care about."

"What if he's bald?" Tag ran a hand through his thick hair.

Leslie's gaze followed his hand. "I think most bald men look sexy."

"Eye color?"

She shook her head. "Doesn't matter to me."

"In shape?"

"Again," she touched a hand to her chest, "it's what's inside that matters."

"You have to narrow it down a little. You know the way this system works." Tag frowned. "Age?"

"Okay, he has to be at least twenty-eight, but I don't mind if he's older than I am," Leslie said. "Older, more mature men can be very sexy."

"Over eighty?"

She smiled. "I'm willing to give it a shot. My grandfather was a very handsome and spry eighty-year-old."

"You'd date your grandfather?" Tag asked, wrinkling his nose.

Leslie sighed. "I don't know. What matters is, that he's kind to animals and people, and that he likes to travel. I don't mind if he drives fast, as long as he's considerate on the highway. No road rage. Austin has some serious traffic issues. I couldn't stand to be stuck in a vehicle with a man who blows a gasket every time he's met with a delay in traffic."

Tag raised a hand. "That rules out a lot of guys, including me."

Leslie laughed. "You never get mad."

"Not with you in the vehicle." He winked. "I don't get mad. It doesn't get me there any faster. If I want to be somewhere at a certain time, I consider the time of day and the traffic patterns."

Tag turned to his monitor and clicked the keyboard. "Must love driving in the country."

"Right?" Leslie chuckled. "Any time I can get outside of the city, I'm happy."

"Me too."

Leslie turned to her monitor. "Likes to cook."

"I can grill a mean steak and chicken breast," Tag said. "Likes to stay home and watch old movies."

"I love old movies," Leslie said. "They have some of the best dialogue."

"I was thinking about the old westerns," Tag drawled.

"Even those had good dialogue," Leslie said. "I love a good Hepburn and Tracy movie." She sighed.

"But I don't just like the oldies. I like a good action adventure or superhero movie. They're just fun."

"I remember you loved the latest Avengers movie," Tag said.

She nodded. "Thanks for taking me. You always seem to know just what I need in the way of entertainment. I think I was feeling down that day. The movie was just what I needed to lift my spirits."

Tag dipped his head. "Glad I could help."

Leslie's mouth twisted. "I feel so comfortable going to a movie with you. It won't be the same with a stranger. I'd feel awkward if he put his arm around me."

"True," he said. "I never know if holding hands on a first date is too much too soon, or not enough too late." Tag chuckled. "And do I kiss her on the first date, or wait for the second or third date?"

Leslie snorted. "Some women would go for the whole enchilada on the first date." She frowned. "That doesn't mean you have to."

He held up his hands. "I don't plan on it. This is supposed to be an effort to find a life mate, not a one-night stand, right?"

She nodded. "That's right. Although some people are only looking for a date. That was Sean and Ava. They only wanted a decent date and look what they got. The whole package." She sighed. "They're perfect for each other."

Tag covered her hand on the mouse. "You're going to find someone perfect for you, too."

She turned her hand over beneath his and squeezed. "I had someone perfect for me. What are the chances of finding it a second time?"

"I believe he's out there. He just might not look like Randy. He might have different but equally appealing qualities. You just have to let Randy go and quit comparing all men to him." He lifted her hand and pressed a kiss to her knuckles. "I get it. He was a great guy, but he's gone. You have a big heart, capable of a whole lotta love. Let yourself love again." He kissed her knuckles again, and then let go of her hand. "Let's get done here. I want to find out who BODS is going to set you up with."

Leslie stared at him a little longer before she turned to the monitor, positioned her fingers on the keyboard and went back to work.

Minutes later, Tag hit the enter key and sat back. "For what it's worth, I'm done."

Leslie nodded and hit the enter key herself. "And so am I." She drew in a deep breath and held it for a moment before letting it out slowly. "I have to admit, I'm a little scared."

Tag laughed. "So am I."

"You are?"

He nodded. "Just think, this could be our last first dates."

"I hadn't thought of that," Leslie said. "That sounds kind of final."

"It also means that it might be the last time we get to go out to dinner together or to a movie, just you and me." Tag gave her a crooked grin. "I think I'll miss that the most."

"What do you mean?" Leslie frowned. "You're not going anywhere, are you?"

"No, but if we find someone else, that someone might not understand us going out together... without them."

Leslie looked down at her keyboard. "You've always been there. Even after Randy and I married. He didn't mind it when you came with us to the movies. We were all friends."

"Not every woman or man will see it that way." He held up his hands. "Just saying. But no use borrowing trouble. We have yet to find a date."

As if on cue, Tag's computer beeped. Leslie and Tag turned to his monitor.

"BODS has found several matches for you," Leslie said, her voice little more than a whisper.

Tag's hand hovered over the mouse.

Leslie's computer beeped.

Tag and Leslie's gazes switched to her monitor.

Leslie's face paled. "I'm not ready for this."

"It won't hurt to see who BODS thinks your perfect match is," Tag said. "You don't have to date any of them." In the back of his mind, he hoped she wouldn't date them. But then she had to find his alter ego and start up a conversation with him. The others would only be people she could compare him against.

She glanced at him, her eyes wide.

"Come on, we can do this," he said. "On three... One... Two... Three." He pressed the enter key at the same time as Leslie. As the monitor blinked, Tag held his breath, praying his plan had worked.

Three profiles came up on Tag's monitor. He shot a glance toward Leslie's monitor. Four profiles came up on hers. Otis Peebles, Herman Lansing and Milton Koch. The last name on the list was Joe Fox.

He let go of the breath he'd been holding. The first phase of his plan had been initiated. His alter ego was one of her candidates, even if his real profile hadn't come up. Now, all she had to do was make contact.

CHAPTER 4

Leslie's hand shook as she cradled the mouse. "Four." She swallowed hard. "That's a lot."

"Make sure you give all four a chance. BODS matched you for a reason."

She leaned over and glanced at his screen. It was easier to concentrate on Tag's matches than on hers.

"I only have three," Tag said.

"Three is better. Less to compare with."

"With my friends, they only had one each. Why so many with us?" Tag asked.

"Because there are more people in the system now," Leslie said. Now, she was wishing she'd done this sooner when there weren't so many. Four was a lot. She shuddered.

"I thought you vetted all your clients," Tag said.

"I run them through a background check before they can go live. They can enter a fake name, but they are required to enter their real one for the background check. I understand how some don't want their real names used right away. Especially if they're very rich. That's the purpose of BODS—to find matches for wealthy clients when their prospective dates don't have any idea of the value of their checking accounts or stock portfolios. And I check that they aren't already married. That was a big deal. I don't want my clients getting involved in extramarital affairs because they trusted my system."

"Good thinking." He looked at her monitor. "So, who've you got, and what are you going to do with them?"

"I thought we'd go through yours first," she said with a smile. "Since your list is shorter." Her smile turned to a grimace. "I'm really procrastinating, but that's to your benefit."

"Okay, but we have to save time to go over your prospects, too," he said.

"We will," she promised. There was no getting out of it, now that she'd committed to testing the waters of the dating pool. "Who's first up?"

"Twyla Stratton," Tag said. "Computer programmer. She likes action-adventure movies, reading science fiction, can ballroom dance and ride horses. Twenty-eight years old, five-feet-six-inches tall, auburn hair and hazel eyes."

"She's pretty and intelligent. You have a common background in computing." Everything Tag could want and more. Leslie's heart constricted. "Sounds good. Worth a first date. What else have you got?"

"Chrissy Trent." Tag squinted at the monitor. "Nurse. Likes old sports cars, runs marathons and triathlons. Loves children. Five-feet-three, blond hair, blue eyes and thirty-four years old."

"She looks ripped," Leslie said, wrapping her arm around her middle, feeling suddenly inadequate. Sure, she worked out, but not like that. Two miles was her limit when she went jogging. "You like to work out. I'm sure you'd find a lot in common. And she loves children." Her heart slipped a little lower in her belly. "Next?"

"Anne Blanchard, technical writer. Loves the outdoors. Enjoys fishing, boating and being outside. Enjoys a good book and quiet nights. Five-feet-nine, brown hair, green eyes."

"She's tall," Leslie pointed out. "And she loves fishing. You love fishing. And you love quiet nights at home, if I recall." She leaned back. "All good. Who will you go out with first?"

"Might as well start at the top with Miss Stratton," Tag said.

"Go ahead, contact her," Leslie urged. "See if she wants to go out with you."

"I didn't think about that. They might not want to go out with me." Tag brought up Twyla and drafted an email through BODS.

Hi, I'm Tag. BODS thinks we're a match. Would you

be interested in going out with me to see if BODS got it right?

"Is that all you have to say?" Leslie shook her head. "Seems so cold and uninviting."

Tag shrugged. "She's on BODS. She should know how it works."

"Yeah, but you have to make her want to go out with you."

"What?" Tag raised his eyebrows. "You wouldn't go out with me after I sent an email like that?"

Again, she crossed her arms over her chest. "No. It was too impersonal. You didn't say what you liked about her profile or what you found interesting about her."

"Too late now. I'll have to wait and see if she rejects me." He nodded toward her monitor. "Let's see who *you* have."

Leslie frowned at the monitor. "Otis...Peebles?" She blinked several times. "Okay...Physicist. So, he's smart. Reads science fiction and action adventure." Leslie nodded. "Goes with the physicist thing."

"He's five-feet-seven."

"Not a problem," Leslie said. "I can still wear heels on a date." She stared at his picture. "He looks nice enough."

"Since your system generates a background check, you know he doesn't have a criminal record. Neither did Jeffrey Dahmer, before he got caught... after killing all seventeen of those men."

"Stop!" Leslie glared at him. "Not everyone is a serial killer."

"True," Tag said. "The problem is, they look like everyone else."

"Seriously, you can't go into this thinking killer."

"And you can't go out with just anyone. You might consider meeting your dates at a restaurant, rather than having them pick you up. That way, you don't have to leave with them."

Leslie stared at the nice-looking man on the screen, suddenly creeped out by the thought of him being a serial killer. "Good point. I'll do that."

"Are you going to go out with him?"

"I don't see why not." She shrugged. "I won't know if he's right for me until I meet him in person."

"What? You don't trust BODS to pick out your mate?" Tag chuckled.

"I do. I just think I'd like to meet him before I decide anything." She clicked on the second man in the lineup.

Tag leaned over her shoulder. "Who's next?"

Tag's nearness caused all kinds of gooseflesh to rise on her arms. If she leaned back just a little, her back would rest against his hard chest. A shiver of desire rippled through her.

"Next?" Tag urged. "Earth to Leslie."

Leslie gave her head a firm shake to snap out of the trance she was falling into. "Next." She squinted at the screen. "Herman Lansing."

"*The* Herman Lansing?" Tag asked.

She lifted a shoulder and let it drop. "That's what the name says on the screen. Should I know him?"

"He's only the wealthiest car dealership owner in all of Texas."

"So?"

"So?" Tag threw his hand in the air. "A man like that has a ton of money. He'll likely spend it on you."

"I don't care about his money. All I care about is his character. Is he nice? Does he care about people and animals?" She shot a glance toward Tag. "If he's none of those things, I want nothing to do with him."

"He's into fitness," Tag said. "He's five-feet-ten and…" He leaned closer to stare at the photo of Herman. "And he's bald."

"Bald can be very attractive," Leslie defended. She stared at the photograph of the smiling man with the shiny head. "Herman is very attractive. He seems confident and fit. I'm sure he's a nice man."

"Moving on," Tag reached around Leslie and commandeered the mouse, clicking on the third candidate. "Milton Koch. Now, here's an interesting man. He's a thriller writer. Likes taking long walks in the woods. Loves to fish and loves nature."

"Oh, my," Leslie said. "He's six-feet-five-inches tall." She shook her head. "That makes him more than a foot taller than me."

Tag chuckled. "Not only can you wear heels with him, you can wear platform heels."

"Again," Leslie said. "How tall or short a man is, does not matter. It's what's in his heart that counts."

"At least, he doesn't sound like a marathon runner. You won't have a hard time keeping up with him if all he likes to do is walk in the woods," Tag said.

He reached around her again, this time brushing her arm with his and sending a shock of awareness throughout her body.

"What about bachelor number four?" He clicked on the link and brought up the guy's profile. "A Mr. Joe Fox."

Leslie leaned closer, staring at the man's photograph. "Oh my, that is an unfortunate picture of him."

"Maybe he's ashamed of his face," Tag said. "Maybe he's tragically pock-marked from a horrible case of acne as a teen. He doesn't want you to know that until after you get to know him online." He raised his hands. "I know. It doesn't matter what he looks like, as long as he's good to the last heartbeat."

"Exactly." She tried to focus on the photo, but it was just too blurry to make out the man's face. "I bet he's kind and considerate."

"He'd have to be, with a face like his," Tag said. "What does his profile say about him?"

Leslie read the data on the monitor. "He says he's six-feet-two."

"That's tall," Tag said.

"But not too tall," Leslie said. "What else?"

"He likes horseback riding," Tag said. "That's got to make you happy."

Leslie nodded. "I like riding horses.

"And horses don't care what your face looks like," Tag said.

"Tag," Leslie said, her tone stern.

Tag grinned. "He likes walking in the rain and dancing cheek to cheek."

"That sounds sweet," Leslie said.

"Ha!" Tag said. "He likes dogs. He doesn't say anything about liking cats."

"That doesn't mean he hates cats," Leslie said.

"Trust me, most guys hate cats," Tag said. "I bet he does, too."

"That's painting guys with a broad stroke." Leslie shook her head. "I bet he likes cats. And he can't be all bad. He likes to dance." She smiled. "Not all guys like to dance."

Tag crossed his arms over his chest. "Now, who's painting guys with a broad stroke?"

Leslie frowned and leaned closer to the monitor. "It says here he wants to get to know me before we meet in person. He's left his email address. That's kind of nice. That way I can get to know him without committing to a one-on-one date."

"Oh, yeah," Tag nodded, "he's definitely a serial killer."

"Stop, already," Leslie said. "He might be just as hesitant to meet someone new as I am. It's hard to commit to a full-on date when you don't know a person."

Tag nodded. "Well, you can start at the top and work your way down the list."

"At the same time, I can start at the bottom and initiate contact with Joe Fox. That way, while I'm getting to know the others on the list, I can get to know Joe." She stared at the monitor. "Why does that name sound familiar?"

"Maybe he's a TV news anchor. Or one of our local movie stars," Tag said.

"Yeah, I don't know where I know that name, but I feel like I do," Leslie said. "I'm sure it will come to me. In the meantime, I'm gonna go ahead and respond to the first guy on the list and see if he's ready to go on a date…I guess. Ugh. I'm so not ready for this."

She rested her hand on the keyboard and tried to think of what to say to a complete stranger.

"It helps if you move your fingers," Tag said with a grin.

"I'm thinking," Leslie said. Nothing came to her. With a quick flourish of her fingers, she keyed:

Hi, I'm Leslie. BODS thinks we're a match. Would you be interested in going out with me to see if BODS got it right?

Tag laughed out loud.

Leslie glared at him.

"It's not easy typing a note to a stranger, is it?"

Leslie sighed. "I should have been more eloquent. I guess it'll be tomorrow before we get a response from our prospective dates."

A pinging sound erupted from her computer monitor.

Tag frowned and leaned over her shoulder. "Looks like you got a response, already."

Leslie clicked the mouse to read the response from Otis.

I'm looking forward to meeting you. How's tomorrow night sound?

Leslie's heart raced, and her gaze met Tag's. "What do I do? What do I do?"

Another ping sounded from Tag's computer monitor.

Leaning over his arm, Leslie pointed at his screen. "Look, yours responded as well." She touched his arm. "See what she said. See what she said."

Tag snickered. "You realize you're repeating yourself, don't you?"

Leslie twisted her hands together. "I don't know what's wrong with me. I never do that. Go on. Go on. See what she said."

Tag read Twyla's message out loud.

You're cute! And yes! I'm available tomorrow night.

"I guess she's going along with your cryptic communications skills," Leslie said.

"Or she's used to texting in short sound bites," Tag said.

"So, are you going?" Leslie asked, her breath catching in her throat. She hadn't seen Tag go out on a date in…well…ever.

"Absolutely." He grinned. "She says I'm cute."

"Good grief," Leslie shook her head. "It's not all about looks. Doesn't she understand that?"

Tag frowned. "Hey, don't knock her. The woman has good taste."

Leslie snorted. "You two deserve each other."

Tag tipped his head toward her monitor. "Are you going out with Otis?"

"I guess so," Leslie said, less than enthusiastic. "It's too bad we can't double date."

Tag raised both hands, palms up. "Who said we couldn't?"

"Wouldn't that be weird?" Leslie asked.

"We could make it look like we're just old friends who bumped into each other," Tag suggested.

Leslie perked up. "Yeah, we could do that. I'd feel much more comfortable if I knew someone was there who had my back."

"Same here," Tag agreed. "Twyla thinks I'm cute. She might jump my bones."

"Please tell me you're not going to sleep with her on your first date," Leslie said.

"Hey, give me a little credit," Tag said. "I promise not to sleep with her…unless she asks me. In which case, I'll go prepared." He winked. "You know, shield the dagger and all."

Leslie slapped his arm. "Eww. I'm going to pretend I didn't just hear that." She shook her head, a smile playing at the corner of her lips. "You're such a jerk."

Tag's grin broadened. "A jerk who doesn't pass up good opportunities. I guess the trick will be to find out where he's taking you."

"I'll let you know as soon as I know. I'll have to know where we're going, if I'm going to meet him there with my own vehicle."

"Right," Tag said. "And you still have the tracking app on your phone, don't you?"

"Yes, I do," she said.

"Then I can keep track of you, if we get separated and he takes you off into the woods to do away with you."

"Seriously, Tag. You're not helping," Leslie said. "I'm unsettled enough as it is." She took a deep breath, her fingers hovering over her keyboard. She lowered them.

Okay. Tomorrow night is good. Where should we meet?

He responded immediately.

Leslie frowned. "He wants to meet at a steak house in Cedar Park."

Tag's brow dipped. "That's northwest of Austin. As long as my date isn't a vegan, we can do it. What time?"

"Kind of early. Six-thirty."

"I'll be there." He keyed a message to Twyla and

had a response back. "She's all for steak, and she wants to meet me there." He clapped his hands together and grinned. "Sounds like we've got dates for tomorrow night."

Leslie wished she could be as excited as Tag. But she wasn't. She'd rather go with *him* to the steak house and be relaxed and comfortable in his company. Instead, she'd be going out on her first date in practically forever, with a complete stranger named Otis.

Tag's hand reached out and covered hers. "It's going to be all right. One date is all you have to do with Otis. If he's not right, you don't have to see him again."

"I know. It's just…" She squeezed his hand. "I'm glad I have you to keep me sane."

"And I'm glad I have you to help me vet my prospects," He lifted her hand to his lips and kissed the backs of her knuckles.

Her heart skipped several beats, and then pounded hard against her ribs. His lips felt soft against her skin. She wondered what they would feel like pressed to her mouth.

"Are you hungry?" he asked, softly.

She licked her lips. "I am."

"Wanna get something to eat?"

"I do," she said, her gaze on his hand holding hers. Then her brain engaged. "No, wait. I can't. I have a meeting tonight with GGC."

"GGC?"

"The Good Grief Club." Her lips twisted. "It's a club some of my friends from grief counseling started to keep in touch with each other after the counseling ended. I'm meeting with them tonight." She tipped her head toward the door. "Ava's a member. And Coop's Emma. Gage's Fiona. She came to the grief therapy group with her father when she lost her mother. That's how we all met. We've been together now for several years."

As if he realized he was still holding her hand, Tag released it and rose to his feet. "Then I won't keep you any longer. I'll see you tomorrow night at the steak house in Cedar Park."

Leslie nodded.

"Do you need me to do anything to shut down the computers?" Tag asked.

"No, thank you." Leslie leaned across and logged him out of the application. "I'll take care of everything." She sighed and met his gaze. "See you tomorrow."

Tag exited the conference room, leaving Leslie alone.

She was just about to log out of her session of BODS when she remembered the fourth candidate, Joe Fox. Quickly, she entered a message.

Hi Joe,

I just wanted to say how refreshing it is to get to know someone via email before actually meeting in person. It helps to alleviate some of the anxiety of face-to-face introductions with perfect strangers.

I'll be honest. I really didn't think I was ready to jump back into the dating pool. You see, I'm a widow...not divorced nor a confirmed bachelorette. I knew what it was like to love someone with my whole heart. I'm afraid anything less will be second best. There, it's out there. I thought you should know what you're up against from the beginning. Not every man is willing to start a relationship in which he must live up to the example set by a ghost.

I'm not always sad, and I have learned to find happiness in every day. One thing that makes me happy is helping others. I love to sing whenever I can. I walk at least a couple of miles a day, and I like an occasional glass of wine. I'm just as happy in the country as I am in the city. Snakes, spiders and critters don't scare me. So, if you love the outdoors, I'm okay with that. If you like sticking with city-life, I'm okay with that as well.

Anyway, I've rambled enough. I hope to hear from you. I'll understand if you don't respond.

Life is short. Have a beautiful day, filled with sunshine and joy.

Leslie

Before she could change her mind, she sent the message, logged out and turned off both computers. What was done was done. She was in BODS, and she had to see it through.

. . .

LESLIE WAS five minutes late when she arrived at the coffee shop where the Good Grief Club met. She always looked forward to the bi-monthly meeting with the circle of friends who'd helped her get through one of the darkest times of her life. She hadn't realized just how long it had taken to enter her profile and Tag's into the BODS system, and then review hers and Tag's matches. She'd pushed the speed limit in order to get to the meeting as close to on time as she could.

When she walked through the door Ava, Emma and Fiona clapped and cheered.

Heat filled her cheeks as she closed the distance between them. "What's all this about?"

Emma grinned. "Ava told us all about it."

"You've come over to the dark side," Fiona said.

Leslie frowned. "What do you mean, the dark side?"

Ava grinned. "You finally jumped into BODS with both feet."

"And all I have to say," Emma said, "is it's about damn time."

"That's right," Fiona agreed. "It's about time you waded out into the dating pool. The rest of us did."

Leslie snorted. "The three of you weren't in the dating pool for that long."

Ava hugged her arms around herself and smiled.

"Yeah, we weren't, were we? But that's the beauty of BODS. Your system got us out of the dating pool so fast we didn't have to drown in one loser after another."

"That's the beauty of the system you designed." Fiona draped an arm around Leslie's shoulder and gave her a quick hug.

As Leslie slid into the booth beside Ava, all three of her friends leaned toward her.

"Now, spill," Emma said.

Leslie hedged. "Why do you want to hear about my day? Emma, you're getting married in three days. We should be talking about the wedding."

Emma shook her head. "The wedding is all under control." She counted off on her fingers. "The dress is ready. Jane's making the cake. I hired a wedding planner to do everything else. All I have to do is show up and get dressed." She looked around the table at her bridesmaids. "You guys are ready, aren't you?"

"I am," Fiona said.

Leslie said, "I have my dress hanging up, ready to go."

"I'm ready as well," Ava said.

Emma turned to Leslie. "So, spill."

"That's right," Fiona said. "We want to know what BODS came up with for you."

Ava grinned. "And we want to know what it came up with for Tag."

Emma's brow twisted. "What's this about the two

of you going into the room together? I thought this was an individual thing."

"I think Tag felt sorry for me," Leslie said. "He agreed to help vet my matches on BODS."

"Matches?" Emma asked. "What do you mean matches?"

"Yeah, right. I only had one," Fiona said.

Ava frowned. "Me, too."

Leslie shrugged. "I left some of the answers vague. Maybe that's why I got more than one match."

"How many did you get?" Emma wanted to know.

"Four," Leslie confessed.

"Four?" Ava exclaimed. "That's a lot."

"I guess it's because we've gotten a lot more entries into the system," Leslie said. "And there are a lot more matches to pull from, now."

"You mean if I'd waited and entered my info today, I might have had three or four different applicants for a date?" Fiona asked.

Leslie shrugged, "Maybe."

Ava, Emma and Fiona all looked at each other.

"Well, I'm glad it ended up the way it did," Ava said. "I couldn't be happier than I am with Sean. And Mica thinks the world of her new daddy."

Emma snorted. "And I couldn't have done better than Coop. He's amazing." She sighed dramatically. "He had my brothers won over on the first date."

"What do you mean he won your brothers over

on your first date?" Fiona asked. "Your brothers went on your first date with Coop?"

"Kinda," Emma said. "I had him come out to the ranch and put him through the cowboy gauntlet. I didn't know he was a rancher himself. I thought he was an accountant, a desk jockey who didn't know one end of a horse from the other. Not only did he know the animals, he helped us haul hay. And he was very good at it. He impressed my brothers from day one." She shook her head. "No, it couldn't have turned out better. And I'm marrying the man I love so much in three days." She smiled.

"Back to the important stuff," Ava said. "Tell us about your potential dates."

Leslie shrugged. "Well there were three I was able to check out all at once, and one who was a little covert."

"What do you mean covert?" Emma asked.

"The first three all had clear pictures and information about themselves so I could make informed decisions about whether or not I wanted to date them."

"And do you?"

Leslie's lips twisted. "There's no reason not to."

"No reason not to?" Emma clucked her tongue. "Were there reasons you should? I mean, did you like what you saw?"

Leslie lifted a shoulder and let it drop. "Pictures never do justice. It's what's inside that counts."

Ava looked at her in horror. "They were all butt-ugly?"

"Not at all," Leslie said. "But looks aren't important. It's what's inside that counts."

"That's what desperate women say," Fiona said. "Honey, you're far from desperate."

Leslie rolled her eyes. "They all looked fine and had a lot going for them on their profiles. I'm going to go out on a date with each of them."

"So, you can pick from the menu?" Ava grinned. "I like it."

"Why did you say the fourth guy was covert?" Emma asked.

Leslie frowned. "His picture was so blurred I couldn't tell what he looked like."

"You said it didn't matter what he looked like," Fiona pointed out.

"True. However, if I was to meet him somewhere, I'd like to know I got the right guy," Leslie said. "Anyway, in his profile, he stated he wanted to communicate via email to get to know me before we met."

Ava, Emma and Fiona exchanged worried glances.

"You sure he's not a serial killer?" Emma asked.

"Oh, for heaven's sake," Leslie exclaimed. "Tag said the same thing."

"Why else would he leave a blurred image of himself?" Ava asked.

Leslie sniffed. "It could be that he's not technically savvy when it comes to webcams and photographs.

He might have moved when the webcam snapped his picture.

"Sounds suspicious to me," Fiona said.

"I'm not too concerned," Leslie said. "It's not like I'll meet him in person right away. We'll get to know each other through email to start with."

"Okay, that's one guy," Emma said. "What's his name?"

"Joe Fox."

Ava frowned. "Joe Fox?"

Leslie nodded. "I know the name sounds familiar, but I can't put my finger on it."

"Joe Fox." Fiona rolled the name around on her tongue. "Joe Fox."

Ava's eyes widened. "Joe Fox. As in Joe Fox from *You Got Mail*?"

"What are you talking about?" Leslie asked.

Emma laughed. "That's right, Ava. *You Got Mail*. The movie with Tom Hanks and Meg Ryan, where he's the big chain bookstore owner, and he puts her little book shop out of business. They met online and were talking to each other without knowing who the other was."

"That's right," Fiona said. "There are like three versions of the story out there. Jimmy Stewart in *The Shop Around the Corner*, and the Judy Garland film, *Good Ol' Summertime*."

Leslie smacked her forehead. "That's where I heard that name. Joe Fox was Tom Hanks's character." She shook her head, a little disappointed. "Why would he do that?"

"Obviously, he doesn't want you to know who he is to begin with," Emma said.

Ava said, "I could dig into the database and find out what his real name is."

Leslie mouth twisted. "I don't know. If I were anyone else on the BODS system, I wouldn't have that kind of access. It doesn't seem fair to dig into the guy's background and find out who he is, until he's ready to let me know."

Emma snorted. "I think you should know up front. What does he have to be ashamed of?"

"Emma, if I recall," Leslie reminded her, "you didn't know who Coop was to begin with. You said it yourself that you thought he was an accountant. If he had told you he was a billionaire and a rancher, you probably wouldn't have gone out with him. Being a billionaire can be a little intimidating on a first date."

Emma's lips twitched. "I would never have guessed he was a billionaire when he first came out to the ranch. He looked just like one of the guys. I think that's what makes Coop, Gage, Sean, Tag and Moose different from other billionaires. They're all real and grounded," Emma said. "They all wanted to find women who were more interested in them than in their bank accounts."

"So, we know you've got Joe Fox. Who are the other three?" Fiona asked.

Leslie gave a brief description of the other three candidates, ending with, "And I have a date tomorrow night with Otis."

"Wow," Ava said. "That was fast."

"Yeah, I kinda agree." Leslie tilted her head to one side. "I'd like to treat them all like Joe Fox. I think I like the idea of getting to know them online before we go through the awkwardness of a first meeting. At least, I'll get to do that with Joe while I check off the other applicants. Hopefully, by the time I've gone out on a date with each of the first three, bachelor number four will be ready to meet in person."

"I understand where you're coming from. It was hard not knowing this person I was supposed to go out on a date with. But it all worked out in the end," Emma said. "I don't have any regrets."

"Neither do I," Fiona said.

"Nor I," said Ava.

"Well, the good thing is that Tag and I have arranged to make it more of a double date," Leslie said.

All three of her friends looked at her, brows raised.

"Really?" Emma asked. "How are you going to do that?"

"I can't imagine any of your BODS clients wanting to go out on a first date with three strangers instead of just one."

"Oh, we're not going to tell them it's a double

date," Leslie said. "He's just going to show up with his date at the same place as my date is taking me. We'll get into a conversation, and then end up sitting together, hopefully."

"Wow," Fiona said. "You're making this more complicated than has to be."

"Even if we don't sit together," Leslie said, "at least he'll be in the same restaurant with me. I won't have to worry about that serial killer taking off with me and dumping my body in a ditch."

Ava nodded. "Good point. Now that I'm thinking about it, I think it's a good idea. You never know who these people are. Just because they pass a background check doesn't mean they haven't committed a crime."

"That's right. It only means they haven't been caught committing a crime," Fiona said.

"That's right," Emma said. "Jeffrey Dahmer killed seventeen men before they caught up with him. He hadn't shown up on a police report before they finally caught him."

Leslie rolled her eyes. "That's what Tag said."

"You know, if you feel more comfortable being around Tag," Emma said, "why don't you date him?"

Heat rose up Leslie's neck into her cheeks. "Tag's been my best friend for so long. He and I and Randy used to go out together before Randy and I got married."

"Why did you choose Randy over Tag?" Ava asked.

Leslie smiled. "I actually loved them both. But Randy was ready to settle down, and so was I. Tag had a lot of maturing to do. I don't think he was ready to get into a long-term relationship."

"And now?" Ava asked.

Leslie's eyes narrowed. "I don't know. I think now he's grown up, and he's ready for a relationship. BODS is going to be a good thing for him. He's a good man. He deserves happiness."

"And you don't?" Emma asked.

"I had happiness with Randy." Leslie smiled.

Emma shook her head. "We all had happiness with our first loves. But it's quite possible to have love again. Don't sell yourself short. Don't die with Randy."

Leslie squared her shoulders and looked her friends in the eyes. "Hey, I entered my name in BODS. I've committed to going out on some dates to meet new people. What more do you want from me?"

"All we want is for you to be happy," Fiona said.

"And to be happy," Emma added, "you have to be open to a new relationship."

Leslie held up her hand as if swearing in court. "I promise I'm going to give it my best shot."

CHAPTER 5

Tag's cellphone rang through his truck's speakers. The caller ID displayed Sean's name. Tag pressed the talk button on his steering wheel. "Hey, Sean."

"Wanna grab a beer with me?"

"Sorry," Tag said. "I have a hot date."

"Wait. What?"

"You heard right. I have a date. I'm on my way to meet her now in Cedar Park."

"Hey, that's good news," Sean said. "Need any advice on what to say and how to act?"

Tag snorted. "No way. All I'll get out of you is sarcasm and bad jokes."

"Seriously, I can tell you all the lines not to say. And the ones that could get you slapped in the face."

"Thanks, but no thanks." Tag chuckled. "I'll take my chances on my own."

"So, who is she?" Sean asked.

Tag shook his head. "No one you'd know."

"I don't know. I used to know a lot of women. Try me."

"I promise, you won't know her. She's a programmer. A technical geek. Her name is Twyla Stratton."

"Okay, you're right. I probably don't know her. I don't remember that name. But I do know a thing or two about dating."

"Yeah, right," Tag said. "You went out one time with Ava, fell in love and now you're happily involved in a relationship."

"I've dated a lot more than you have, buddy. I just didn't find the right person until I met Ava. My main advice to you is don't settle. When you meet the right person, you'll know. And stick with that woman until you convince her that you're the right person for her."

Oh, he knew who the right person was for him. He had her in mind already. He just had to convince Leslie that he was the right person for her.

"Well, don't let me keep you away from your love life," Sean said. "Just think, this Twyla woman could be the future Mrs. Bronson."

Not a chance, Tag thought. "I hope you find someone to catch a beer with."

"Let me know how it goes," Sean said. "Later, dude."

Tag arrived at the steakhouse five minutes early. His plan was to meet Twyla at the door at exactly six-thirty. He searched the parking lot for Leslie's white Lexus SUV and didn't see it. He frowned. It wasn't like Leslie to be late. She was usually fifteen minutes early to everything.

An auburn-haired woman climbed out of a silver DeLorean. She wore a royal blue dress with a black waistband that had white lettering that read Police Public Call Box on it. She looked like she was wearing a Tardis from the *Dr. Who* television show.

Tag studied her face. She looked like the woman from the picture he remembered on BODS. He glanced at the parking lot one last time before getting out of his truck. Leslie still hadn't arrived. All of a sudden, Tag was feeling awkward about meeting this woman he knew nothing about. All along, he'd only been concerned about being there when Leslie arrived, not to get to know Twyla Stratton. He squared his shoulders. He'd promised the woman a date, and he had to live up to that promise. As he walked across the pavement, a white Lexus SUV skidded sideways into the parking lot and came to a shuddering halt.

"What the hell?" Tag frowned.

Leslie never drove fast or recklessly.

She backed into a parking slot and climbed out of her vehicle.

"Hi, you must be Tag Bronson," a voice said beside him.

Tag dragged his gaze away from the white Lexus

and glanced at the auburn-haired woman. "And you must be Twyla Stratton."

She nodded, her gaze taking him in from head to toe. "It's a good thing you look like your photo. I was afraid I wouldn't recognize you."

He smiled and glanced at her dress. "Dr. Who fan?"

She grinned and nodded. "Guilty. I did put in my profile that I'm a sci-fi geek. I guess I was putting it mildly. I hope that doesn't bother you. I like to think of myself as quirky, not crazy."

Tag gave her a reassuring smile. "That's good to know. I like action adventure and science fiction movies and books. I thoroughly enjoyed all the Star Wars and Star Trek franchise offerings."

She let out a heartfelt sigh. "Good. Then we'll have something in common."

"Tag?" a voice said behind him. "Tag, is that you?"

Tag's pulse pounded. He turned to face Leslie as she crossed the parking lot, wearing a bright red sundress with narrow spaghetti straps that complemented her sandy-blond hair.

He played along with the ruse. "Leslie?"

She laughed. The sound was strained and nervous to Tag but probably not noticeable to anyone else. "Fancy meeting you here," she said.

Tag smiled. "What brings you out to Cedar Park?"

She glanced around the parking lot. "I'm here to meet a date."

A short man wearing dark trousers, a white shirt and a bow tie got out of his sedan and walked toward Leslie.

Based on what Tag recalled from his picture on the BODS application, this had to be Otis Peebles.

Leslie turned toward to him with a smile and held out her hand. "Are you Otis Peebles?"

"I am," he said and took her hand. "And you must be Leslie Lamb."

"I am. Nice to meet you, Otis." She turned toward Tag. "I just ran into an old friend. Otis, this is Tag Bronson. Tag, Otis Peebles, my date."

Tag took the man's hand, even though Otis's grip was limp with no bones or muscle behind it. He gave the man a firm shake and nodded. "Nice to meet you." He turned toward his date. "And this is Twyla Stratton, my date. Twyla, this is Leslie Lamb and Otis Peebles."

Twyla held out her hand to Leslie and shook it briefly. "Nice to meet you." Then she turned her attention to Otis, her eyes narrowing on his bow tie. "Oh, my gosh! Is that a Dr. Who bowtie?"

Otis laughed and touched his fingers to the tie. "Yes, it is. It's one of my favorites. I love the concept of the Tardis being a time machine. This was the only bow tie I could find with the Tardis on it."

Leslie laughed softly. "Look at you two. Your outfits match."

Twyla held out her hand to Otis. "So very nice to meet you, Otis."

He gripped her hand and smiled into her eyes. "So nice to meet you, too, Twyla."

Tag dove into his opportunity. "Since you two match, and Leslie and I know each other, why don't we sit together in the restaurant?"

Otis shot a glance toward Leslie. "Are you okay with that?"

She nodded. "Absolutely. You two obviously have something in common, and Tag and I are old friends. That'll make us all more comfortable getting to know each other."

"My reservation was for a table for two," Otis said.

Tag held up a hand. "I'll take care of it when we get inside. I'm sure they have a table for four."

"I don't know," Otis said, his brow wrinkling. "They book up pretty quickly. I was lucky to get a table for tonight."

Otis held the door for Twyla and Leslie.

Tag took over and held the door for Otis. Once inside, Tag excused himself with, "I'll see what they have." He left the other three standing by the door and crossed to the hostess's stand. He'd already reserved a table for four. He let the hostess know they were there, and that Otis Peebles's reservation could be canceled.

Tag rejoined the others. "We're in luck," he said. "They were able to give us a table for four."

Otis smiled. "That's perfect." He turned to Leslie. "Are you a fan of *Dr. Who*?"

"I've watched a few of the shows," Leslie admitted.

Otis blinked several times. "A few?"

Leslie grimaced. "Sorry. I…uh…don't get much of a chance to watch TV. I do like action-adventure and superhero movies, as well as science fiction stories, like *Star Trek* and *Star Wars*."

"Oh, okay." Otis turned toward Twyla. "I take it you're a Dr. Who fan, too?"

Twyla laughed. "What was your first clue?"

"I really like the Tardis dress." He smiled at Twyla. "And who was your favorite Dr. Who?"

She snorted "In my opinion, there was only one Dr. Who, and that was David Tenant."

"That goes without saying," Otis said. "Although, I must admit I was impressed with Peter Capaldi, who played Dr. Who from 2013 through 2017. He started out a little rough, but he got good after a while."

Twyla nodded. "Agreed. But still, David Tenant was the man."

"If you'll follow me, I'll get you seated," the hostess said, carrying a stack of menus.

Otis returned his attention to Leslie and held out his arm.

She slipped her hand into the crook of his elbow, her gaze going to Tag.

Tag's gut knotted just a little. He knew this was her date with Otis. Tag held out his arm for Twyla.

She hooked her arm through his. Together, they wound their way through the steakhouse and took their seats, boy-girl, boy-girl.

Though Tag wasn't with Leslie on this date, he at least got to sit beside her, with Leslie on one side and Twyla on the other.

As they settled at the table, Leslie turned to Otis and smiled. "I noticed on your profile that you're a physicist."

Otis nodded. "I am."

"What exactly does a physicist do?"

Otis smiled. "I work at the University of Texas in Austin as a research physicist. I design experiments to test theories. We use the scientific method and draw conclusions about the theories."

"That sounds very interesting," Leslie said. "What do you like to do when you're not at work?"

Otis glanced toward Twyla. He hesitated for a moment, and then he launched into his after-hours activities. "I am such a fan of sci-fi movies about comic book heroes."

"Seriously?" Twyla said. "Did you know that there's a Comic Con here in Cedar Park this weekend?"

"As a matter of fact, I did know," Otis said, looking back at Leslie as if he was about to say more.

The waitress chose that moment to take their orders. After she left, Twyla and Otis got into a discussion about the Comic Con and which celebrities would be in attendance. They continued with a detailed discussion of several episodes of *Dr. Who*.

Tag caught Leslie's gaze, his mouth twitching at the corners.

Otis finally remembered he was on a date with Leslie. He turned to her. "And what do you like to do in your off hours? For that matter, what is it you actually do?"

She smiled. "I'm a software developer."

Twyla perked up. "Really? I'm a programmer."

Leslie turned to Tag. "Tag is a software developer, as well." Thankfully she didn't mention that his software firm was international, and that he made a lot of money at it. Leslie understood the importance of keeping her clients' monetary status confidential. People tended to treat him differently when they knew how much he was worth.

"What kind of programming do you do?" Otis asked Twyla.

"I do programming for medical experiments for clinical research projects," she replied.

"That's interesting," Otis said with a smile. "How long have you been doing that?"

"I landed the job straight out of college. I've been at it now for the past seven years." She shrugged. "It's interesting work, and I enjoy being involved in the trials. I hope that someday I'll be involved in a clinical trial that will be responsible for finding the cure for cancer."

Otis nodded. "That would be the ultimate victory." He turned to Leslie. "What kind of software do you develop?"

"Relational database software," Leslie said, her gaze capturing Tag's, her lips quirking upward in a smile.

Tag almost snorted out of his nose the drink he'd been sipping. More like relationship software. Her clients didn't need to know she was the one responsible for the BODS system that got them there.

Thankfully, their food arrived, limiting the amount of talking they could do. Tag ate his steak, watching as Leslie pushed hers around on her plate. He'd make certain she got a box to take her meal home to eat later. The woman didn't eat nearly enough.

When she became his wife, he'd take better care of her. He liked cooking and didn't mind cleaning. He had a maid that did both, but he still preferred to do his own chores.

After their plates were cleared away, Leslie pushed back from the table. "If you'll excuse me, I'd like to make a visit to the ladies' room."

Tag waited a few moments then stood. "Excuse me. I need to see a man about a horse."

Twyla's brow scrunched. "A horse?"

Otis chuckled. "He's going to the restroom."

Twyla's eyes widened. "Oh."

He hurried to the rear of the restaurant where the

restrooms were located down a narrow hallway. Though he didn't need to use the facilities, he wanted to compare notes with Leslie about their dates. He waited outside the ladies' room until she emerged.

Her eyes widened when she saw him.

He smiled. "So, what do you think about Otis?"

Leslie looked in both directions to make certain Otis and Twyla weren't coming or going in the hallway. She smiled up at Tag. "I think he's a very nice man. He's intelligent, not bad looking, and he knows a lot about Dr. Who and celebrities." She shrugged. "I guess I need to brush up on my *Dr. Who* series if I plan on seeing him again."

Tag frowned. "Are you planning on seeing him again?"

She shrugged again. "I don't know. I want to give the other candidates a chance before I decide."

Tag nodded. "The big question is, can you see Otis as the father of your children?"

Leslie's brow puckered. "I don't know. It's hard to say after just one date." She raised her eyebrows. "How about you? Twyla is pretty, and she's very sweet and smart."

"You say that as if you don't expect me to date a smart woman," Tag said.

"Not at all," Leslie said. "You're a very smart man. I'd expect you to date someone equally smart. Otherwise, you'd walk all over her."

"And that's why I like you so much," Tag said. "You

call it like it is, and you don't let me get away with anything."

She grinned. "What are friends for, if they can't tell you the truth?" She tilted her head. "So, do you see Twyla as the mother of your four children?"

There was no way in hell he'd marry Twyla, but Tag played along. "She's nice. She's good-looking, and she'd make pretty babies. But I can't see me marrying a woman who'd probably want to name a child Dr. Who, or after David Tenant, Spock, Spider Man or Thor." He lifted a shoulder. "And I'm not all that into Comic Cons or cosplay. Dressing up is fun for Halloween parties or masquerade balls, but I'm not all that into it. I'd feel more comfortable riding a horse out on my ranch."

"Exactly," Leslie said. "Fewer people...wide open spaces...communing with nature." She sighed. "Sounds like heaven."

"It is," he said. "Especially when you can share it with someone who appreciates it equally."

Leslie glanced down the hallway. "I guess we should head back before they come looking for us."

Tag nodded. He started to go around her in the hallway when a woman exited the ladies' room and bumped into him. Tag pitched toward Leslie, catching himself by bracing his arms on the wall on either side of Leslie.

"Sorry," the woman said and hurried away.

Tag wasn't sorry. He was right where he'd always

wanted to be...his body pressed against hers. Everywhere they touched was on fire. He could feel the heat burning through him.

Leslie's irises flared. She tilted her head up toward his. All he had to do was dip his chin just a little and he could capture her mouth with his.

A large man entered the narrow hallway. "Excuse me," he said.

Tag didn't want to move, but he had to in order to let the man get by to the men's room.

He'd been so very close to kissing her. Once again, he told himself, it was too soon, He wondered if it wasn't too soon to let her know it was a possibility. He wanted to give her something to keep in mind on her dates. Not that he wanted her kissing her dates. But if the opportunity came up, how would she feel about kissing Otis as compared to him?

"We'd better get back to our dates," Leslie said.

Tag nodded and moved out of the way, allowing the big guy to move past them. He cupped Leslie's elbow and guided her down the hallway until they reached the end of the corridor.

"You'd better go before me," Tag said.

She nodded and took off across the room.

Tag followed a few seconds later. When he arrived at the table, Otis and Twyla were grinning. "We just had a great thought," Otis said and cast a quick glance in Twyla's direction. "We are just around the corner from Greater Austin's Comic Con. They stay open until ten o'clock. Let's go."

Tag really didn't want to go, but when he looked at the pained expression in Leslie's eyes, he smiled. "Great idea. Let's do it."

For the next three hours, he, Leslie, Twyla and Otis walked around the convention center, bumping into numerous versions of Thor, Spider Man and nearly naked women dressed as Princess Leia or Wonder Woman. It worked out well for Tag, because he got to walk with Leslie, while Twyla and Otis bonded over a life-size Tardis parked in the middle of the convention center. They snapped photos of each other in front of the big blue box, and with other cosplay characters, having the time of their lives.

Tag leaned toward Leslie. "Having fun?"

Leslie tilted her head to the side a little. "Actually, I am."

Tag frowned. "Really? I didn't think this was your scene."

"I didn't either," Leslie said. "But I find it fun watching other people enjoying it so much. Who knew I'd be a fan of Comic Con? I definitely need to read up on my comic books, watch my action movies and catch up on *Dr. Who*, if I decide to see Otis again."

Tag nodded toward Twyla and Otis. "You may have some competition in Twyla."

Leslie smiled. "They do seem to be getting along quite well, don't they?"

"They have a lot in common, starting with their clothing," Tag said.

Leslie glanced down at her sleek gray slacks and soft white blouse. Then she looked at Tag's dark jeans and white button-down shirt. "We don't really fit in here, do we?" she said.

"Not really," he said. "We might be considered boring compared to the others in the convention center."

"That's okay," Leslie said. "But I do like the bright blue Tardis dress Twyla is wearing. Royal blue is one of my colors."

Tag leaned back and stared at her. "Seriously? I only ever see you wearing gray."

She grinned. "That's my professional look."

"And when are you not professional?"

She shrugged and grinned. "When I'm wearing my PJs at home."

"Now, you have me curious," he said. "What do your PJs look like?" His groin tightened at the thought of Leslie in her PJs.

"That's my little secret," Leslie said. "It's one of my guilty pleasures."

"Was is something between you and Randy?" he asked, maybe a little jealous of his best friend and ghost.

She shook her head. "No. I started buying crazy

pajamas after Randy passed. It helped to make me happy when I was at my saddest. Emma bought me my first pair. It had a pattern of rainbows and unicorns. It had a logo on it that said, 'If you can be anything in this world, be a unicorn. Be proud of being different.'"

Tag looked around the convention center with a smile. "I think we have a lot of unicorns in this room."

"Yes, indeed, we do. And they are all proud of their individualism. Next time we come, we're dressing up."

"We?" Tag's eyebrows rose.

"Being here brings something important to my attention," she said.

"Brings what to your attention?" he asked.

"That we don't play enough."

Tag smiled. "Aren't we a little old to be playing?"

Leslie shook her head. "Never."

"This is a side of you that I don't remember," Tag said.

"Probably because, with everything that has happened over the past ten years, I've forgotten how to play. If we hadn't come on this date tonight, I wouldn't have remembered. And if things don't work out with Otis," Leslie said, "I still need to thank him."

"For what?" Tag asked.

"For reminding me how to be young. For reminding me that just because you're an adult, you don't have to grow up. You can still be a functioning, contributing member of society and still play."

"I like that," Tag said. "I like that a lot. And I like you."

They stayed until the doors closed. Since they brought their own cars, they ended up leaving at the same time.

Otis shook hands with Twyla and Tag, and then turned to Leslie and held her hands in his, smiling at her. "Thank you, Leslie. I really enjoyed the evening."

Leslie returned his smile, making Tag's gut clench. "Thank you, Otis. I enjoyed it, too."

Tag turned to Twyla. "Twyla, it's been a pleasure."

Twyla smiled up at him. "I really appreciate you bringing me here tonight. And thank you for introducing me to your friends." She shot a smile toward Otis. "I can't remember a better double date than I had tonight. And I wasn't looking forward to this date, thinking I would have nothing in common with you."

Tag tipped his head a bit. "Actually, you didn't have as much in common with me, as I would have expected."

"Yeah, but you were nice enough to let me be me. And I appreciate that." She leaned up on her toes and planted a kiss on his cheek. "Thank you again."

Otis saw Leslie to her car.

Even though Tag would have liked to see Leslie to

her car, he waited until Twyla got in her car and drove away.

Once Leslie drove her car out of the parking lot, Tag waved to Otis, climbed into his truck and drove home. He hadn't gone very far before he dialed Leslie's number on his cellphone.

"What? She didn't insist on sleeping with you tonight?" Leslie asked without preamble.

Tag laughed. "I think she would rather have slept with Otis."

"You're right," Leslie said. "Those two were too cute. Are you disappointed?"

"Not at all," he said. "I got to spend the evening with you."

"That wasn't exactly how it was supposed to end up, but I'm glad too," Leslie said. "Although I liked Otis, I like being with you better."

Tag's chest swelled. "I'm glad to hear it, since the feeling is mutual. Want me to follow you home?"

"That's not necessary," she said. "I know you have a long drive to your ranch."

"I don't mind at all," Tag said. "And I'm not going to the ranch tonight. I'm staying in town at my penthouse."

"It's not necessary to follow me home," she said. "But you can talk to me along the drive there."

"Deal," he said.

For the rest of the drive, they talked about the

people they saw at Comic Con, about the steak and anything else that came up.

She talked to him all the way to her home and into her house until she locked the door. "Goodnight, Tag," she said. "I hope you sleep well."

"Sweet dreams, Leslie," he said and ended the call. "I love you." He hoped that, someday soon, he'd be able to say that to her out loud.

CHAPTER 6

BEFORE SHE'D TAKEN two steps into her house, Leslie's phone rang again. Thinking it might be Tag, she answered it quickly. "Hey there, miss me already?"

Emma's voice came through the receiver. "Wow, Leslie, was your date that good?"

Leslie's face burned. "Oh. Hi, Emma. I thought you were someone else."

"Obviously," Emma said. "How was Otis? It was Otis, right?"

"Actually, the date with Otis was kind of different," Leslie admitted.

"Tell me about it," Emma urged.

Leslie walked through her house slowly, talking to Emma, telling her about the evening, the double date, Otis and Twyla hitting it off, and then ending up at Comic Con.

"So, you and Otis didn't hit it off. But it sounds like you and Tag got along great."

Leslie smiled at the image of him walking with her at Comic Con. "Actually, we did. He's a really good friend."

Emma snorted. "Friend? You guys have been as thick as thieves since you got BODS started. Why aren't you two a thing?"

"To be honest, I've been asking myself the same question," Leslie admitted. "I guess it's because Tag and Randy were the best of friends. When I think about Tag as anything other than a friend, I feel like I'm being disloyal to Randy."

"That's bullshit," Emma said. "Randy's not here anymore, Leslie. You gotta live your life. And if your life includes Tag, all the better. Randy would have blessed the relationship. He loved Tag like a brother and would have been happy to know that he was taking care of you."

"Maybe so, but it still feels weird." Leslie dropped her purse on her kitchen counter. "Besides, I have three more guys to go through that BODS matched me with. And BODS can't be wrong, can it?"

"Well, it worked for four of us," Emma said. "It wouldn't hurt to give the other three men a try."

"That's the plan," Leslie said.

"And while you're at it, remember," Emma said, "a bird in the hand is worth three in the bush."

Leslie's brow dipped, and a smile played at the corners of her mouth. "Does that make Tag a bird?"

"Read into it what you will." Emma chuckled. "I think Tag is a great guy. And I think he thinks you're a great gal."

"Yeah, but what if he only thinks of me as a friend? I don't want to do anything to ruin our friendship."

"It doesn't hurt to keep your options open," Emma said. "Have a good night. I love you, girl."

"I love you, too, Emma." Leslie ended the call, got dressed in her unicorn pajamas, crawled into bed and pulled out her laptop. She logged into the BODS application to make sure it was up. Then she logged into her account to look at her next candidate. As soon as she logged in, a bell chimed, and a message came up from Joe Fox. She opened it eagerly.

Dear Leslie,

I'm glad you didn't find my method of getting to know each other off-putting. I'm also glad you were honest about how you feel about dating. I'm sorry you lost your husband whom you loved dearly. He must have been a wonderful man. The fact that you loved him so much shows your capacity for love and gives me hope that there is a woman out there who could love me as much as you loved your husband. I would never ask you to compare me to your first husband, but to at least be open to the possibility that there might be someone out there you could love in a different way. You're obviously a very caring and loving individual. I find that refreshing and hopeful. I, too, like to sing, but I do that in the shower, so nobody has to listen to me in my toneless wonder. I also love to walk. I like to ride horses as well, and I enjoy a good glass of wine, although I prefer a beer on a hot day. Though I spend a lot of time in the city, my heart is in the country. I don't mind the spiders and snakes and critters. They are all a part of life. I love when I can stare up at the sky and see the stars, without the city lights around me. I love it even more when I can share the wonders of heaven with someone I care about. Thank you for responding to my rambling. You did fill my day with sunshine and joy. I wish you the same.

Joe

LESLIE'S first reaction was to pick up the phone and call Tag. She paused, though. Her messages with Joe seemed more personal. She shouldn't share them with anyone else, even Tag, who was her best friend. Instead, she wrapped her arms around her middle and gave herself a hug. The evening had gone a lot better than she'd anticipated. She'd liked Otis, she'd liked Twyla. She'd liked that they'd gotten along with each other. And she'd enjoyed her time with Tag. Any time with Tag was always good. As she thought about the moment they'd stood in the hallway outside the bathrooms in the steakhouse, she trembled. When he'd leaned close to her, she'd sworn he was going to kiss her. She wished he had. Now, looking down at the letter from Joe, she wondered. Was Tag the one she was meant to be with after Randy? Or was there someone else out there?

She sighed, closed her computer and turned out the light. As she lay on her pillow, she was more confused than when she'd first signed on to BODS.

As soon as Tag got home, he hurried to his computer and logged into the BODS application. He'd sent his message to Leslie right before he'd left for his date with Twyla, knowing Leslie wouldn't receive it until she got home that evening. She would have read the message by now. His heart beat fast as he pulled up his messages within the BODS system. As he had expected, Leslie had received and read the note. He had wondered if she would say anything to him about Joe Fox, Bachelor Number Four. He picked up his cellphone and dialed her number.

After several rings, she answered, "Hello?"

"Hey, beautiful. Did I wake you?"

"Oh, hey, Tag. No, I wasn't quite asleep yet. I'd just laid my head on the pillow when your call came through."

"Good. Then I guess you want to talk about how things went tonight with our dates…?" Tag suggested.

"We already discussed most of the evening on our way home. What more do we need to talk about?"

"Not much. I thought it was funny how Otis and Twyla hit it off right away."

Leslie laughed. "How interesting that they were both *Dr. Who* fans. What are the chances that they hit it off with each other, and not with us? I'm not so sure BODS hit the mark on these matches."

"Do you get the feeling fate played a part in this?" Tag asked.

Leslie answered softly, "I do."

"Would you be disappointed?" Tag asked.

"If they get together?" Leslie asked.

"Yes," Tag said.

"How could I be disappointed? I just want them to be happy. They seem so perfect together." Leslie paused. "Are you disappointed? I mean Twyla was cute, engaging and had beautiful auburn hair. You two could have a lot more in common than you think."

"Though she was cute, and she was sweet and entertaining, she's not really my type," Tag said. "I'm not as into sci-fi as she is, nor would I be as willing to follow every Comic Con convention around the country dressed as Thor or as a captain of a starship."

Leslie's chuckle sounded in his ear. "I can just picture you dressed as Thor, wearing a cape and carrying a big plastic hammer."

Tag snorted.

"What?" Leslie paused. "You don't see yourself as a superhero?"

"Not hardly."

Leslie sighed. "The way I see it, superheroes don't have to have superpowers to be so super or to be heroes. I think a person being in the right place at the right time, doing the right thing makes him a hero."

"So, have you thought about it? Do you see yourself going out with Otis again?" he asked.

"I don't know if you noticed," Leslie said, "but I thought I saw Otis and Twyla exchanging phone numbers."

Tag laughed. "What do you want to bet they go to the Comic Con in Cedar Park tomorrow and spend the entire day together?"

"That would be my guess."

"Speaking of tomorrow, we're heading into Emma and Coop's wedding weekend. Are you ready for the rehearsal dinner?"

"I'm ready. Are you?" Leslie asked.

"I'm not much into weddings, rehearsals or rehearsal dinners. But Coop's my friend, and I do look forward to him marrying Emma. Those two were made for each other. I couldn't be happier for them."

"Me, too," Leslie said, her voice soft. "Emma deserves some happiness. Losing her fiancé nearly killed her. Now that she's found Coop, I've never seen her happier."

"You're still my plus one for the rehearsal,

rehearsal dinner and the wedding, aren't you?" Tag asked.

"Of course."

"You didn't ask Otis to stand in for you, did you?" Tag teased.

"Even had I asked, I'm sure he would have declined the honor," Leslie said. "I mean, when you have a choice between Comic Con and a stranger's wedding, Comic Con would win out every time. Especially with Otis."

"True," Tag said.

"You're not bringing Twyla, are you?"

"Like you said, I'm betting they're going to Comic Con tomorrow. Besides, I promised to take you to Coop's wedding. You're my plus one. That makes me all yours."

Leslie laughed. "I'd be going anyway. I'm one of Emma's bridesmaids."

"True. But if you're my plus one, I get to claim first dance."

"Is that how it works?" Leslie asked, a little breathlessly.

"Yup," Tag said. "That's how it works."

"Good. Then I get to test your ballroom dancing lessons to see if they took."

"You're on," Tag said. "I'll pick you up at your place tomorrow afternoon. Five o'clock?"

"Five o'clock should give me enough time to change and for us to get to the rehearsal at 6:00 pm."

Leslie chuckled. "I think it's funny they settled on getting married in a church in Hellfire, Texas. It should make for a good start to an exciting union."

"I like that the rehearsal dinner and afterparty will be at the Ugly Stick Saloon." Tag was really looking forward to that. "How are you at two-stepping?"

Leslie chuckled. "I haven't been two-stepping in years. I'm not sure I remember how."

"I'll show you." For someone who didn't particularly care for all the hoopla of wedding rehearsals, Tag was looking forward to the whole weekend with her. He hadn't danced with Leslie since her wedding to Randy. He looked forward to holding her in his arms with the good excuse of dancing. And dancing, if done right, could be almost as sensual as making love.

"Then I'll see you tomorrow?" she asked.

"I can't wait," he replied.

"Goodnight, Tag."

"'Night, darlin'." He ended the call and sat for a moment, staring at his cellphone. Leslie hadn't mentioned the message from Bachelor Number Four. He wondered if she'd mention it tomorrow. He wondered if she'd mention it at all, or if she was keeping that little secret to herself.

Tag wasn't sure how he felt about that. He thought he and Leslie were sharing practically everything. That she wasn't sharing her thoughts about Joe

Fox gave him pause. Hell, he was jealous of the man —and he *was* Bachelor Number Four.

Tag slipped out of his clothes and laid naked on his bed, staring up at the ceiling. Though everything was going as planned, he was left with an unsettled feeling. He'd thought his plan foolproof.

The players in this game were human. As a software developer of a multi-million-dollar company, he knew that when you injected humans into a plan, anything could happen. Humans were the wild card. At least Leslie wasn't all that taken with Otis. That didn't mean she wouldn't find the other two candidates to her liking.

Tag had to make sure he was there every time. He hoped that, eventually, she'd come to the conclusion he was the right one for her, not the others. If he had to do that through Joe Fox, so be it.

CHAPTER 7

Ava plopped down in the chair across from Leslie's desk in her office the next day. "Oh, my gosh. Could the day have been any more hectic?"

Leslie laughed. "It's Friday. It's as if all our BODS clients get anxious if they don't have a date by Friday night. Everyone starts calling the help line, as you can tell, wondering if the system is down."

"I haven't had a single moment to sit down and ask you how your date went last night." Ava stared across the desk, her eyebrows raised.

"Wow, I hadn't even thought about it all day long." Leslie knew it was a half-truth. She was okay with that. She'd thought about last night, but not about her date with Otis. Her thoughts went to that narrow hallway in the steakhouse and the almost-kiss from Tag. And then she'd thought about her message from Joe and her need to respond to him before this night was over. At least five times she'd started typing her response, only to scrap everything she'd keyed. Her words didn't seem adequate, not after Joe's eloquent and meaningful message to her. She'd come to the conclusion they'd done all the introduction they needed to find out about each other. Now, they needed to move on and find out a little more about each other in the form of the future and their expectations of life.

What she'd share with him, she hadn't a clue. She couldn't tell him her plans for BODS. He couldn't know she was the brains behind the matchmaking system. If he knew, then he'd know she had access to his personal data, and that she could know who he really was. And why wouldn't he think she'd do that? She wanted him to trust her and share whatever he felt he needed to share with her. At this point, if she told him who she was, and that she was behind BODS, that would ruin everything.

And at that moment, she didn't want things to end between her and Joe, even though, technically, nothing had actually started.

"Your date was that good?" Ava crossed her arms over her chest, giving Leslie a pointed look.

Leslie shook her head. "Sorry, I must be woolgathering again."

"So how was it?" Ava asked. "Did you manage to finagle a double date with Tag and his date?"

"Went off without a hitch," Leslie said with a smile. "Tag was so smooth."

Ava grinned. "Well, did you enjoy the evening?"

"Actually, I did." Leslie stared out the window, as if staring into her memories. "My date was very nice. Tag's date was, too."

"That tells me a whole lot," she said, her tone wry.

Leslie looked back at Ava. "Otis is a *Dr. Who* fan and a physicist.

Ava nodded. "We got that much from BODS. The *Dr. Who* fan part of his personality…that is different." Ava frowned. "That could be a good thing or a bad thing."

"How could it be bad?" Leslie asked.

Ava shrugged. "Some people get fanatical about being fans. They get into the cosplay. Some of them believe they're the characters they portray."

Leslie frowned. "I think Otis just enjoys the whole Comic Con scene. And, get this, Tag's date Twyla was all into the same. She showed up in a Tardis-blue dress that matched Otis's Tardis-blue bowtie."

Ava's eyes widened. "You've got to be kidding me. Sounds like your dates were meant to be together."

"That's the conclusion Tag and I came to." Leslie smiled. "We ate at a table for four at the steakhouse. Afterward, we went to the Comic Con convention in Cedar Park. Otis and Twyla were in their element. They talked to everyone in costume and even those who weren't, who were celebrities who acted in some of those shows." Leslie smiled. "Tag and I followed behind them."

"What you're telling me is that you switched dates," Ava said.

"No," Leslie shook her head. "We were still with our original dates. I was with Otis. Tag was with Twyla. At the end of the night, we said our good-nights to our respective dates."

"Did you arrange for a second date with Otis?" Ava asked.

Leslie's lips twisted. "I kinda don't think Otis wants to go out with me again. He was much more interested in Twyla than me."

Ava chuckled. "Of course, he was. As one *Dr. Who* fan to another, they had a lot more in common with each other than with you and Tag."

Leslie nodded. "Yes, they did. And they were so cute together. I'm happy for them. If ever a couple belongs together, it's Twyla and Otis."

Ava nodded. "And, once again, you and Tag were left alone for the evening."

Leslie frowned. "We didn't stick around. After the date was over, we all went our separate ways."

"So, you didn't get together with Tag and compare notes about your respective dates?"

Leslie grimaced. "Well…"

"Ha!" Ava grinned. "So, you did compare notes."

Leslie sighed. "We did. All the way home by cellphone. And when we got home, he called again to discuss today's events."

She arched an eyebrow. "And was he taken with Miss Twyla?"

Leslie smiled. "About as much as I was taken with Otis."

"And were you taken with Otis? Were you disappointed that he and Twyla got along so well together?"

Leslie shook her head. "Not at all. Otis was a nice man. He's charming. He was considerate." She paused. "And he was very much into Twyla." Leslie raised her hands palms upward. "Like I said, I'm happy for them. In a roundabout way, BODS was the system that introduced them. Through Tag and me."

"Well, I still think you need to consider dating Tag," Ava said.

Leslie frowned. "I can't date Tag. He was my husband's best friend. That just seems wrong."

"There's nothing wrong with going out with Tag," her friend said. "He's good-looking as all get out. You know each other inside and out. And you like each other."

"But is that enough basis to date?" Leslie asked. "Aren't forever relationships based on love?"

"So? Why can't you love Tag?"

Leslie rose from her chair, walked to the floor-to-ceiling windows and stared outside. "I don't know. I just don't know. It seems wrong, even when it feels right."

Ava snorted. "Uh-huh. I thought there was something between you and Tag."

Leslie spun to face Ava. "Oh, you cannot say anything to Tag."

Ava held up her hands. "Don't worry. I'm not going to do anything stupid."

"It's just that I've had these feelings. Twice now, he's been close enough for me to kiss him." Leslie's cheeks heated. "And I wanted him to."

Ava leaped out of her chair and crossed the floor to stand in front of Leslie. She gripped her arms and stared into her face. "Leslie, you of all people know that life is short. You have to grab for the joy. You can't let it get by. You want to go to your grave with no regrets."

"When Randy knew he was dying and only had a couple of days to live, he made me promise not to grieve for too long." Leslie stared into Ava's eyes. "How long is too long?"

"Randy's been dead for four years. Too long would have been about two years ago," Ava said. She pulled Leslie into her arms and hugged her tight. "You really need to get on with your life. And you can't let a little thing like Tag being your husband's best friend slow you down. Randy would have approved of Tag being more than just a friend to you. He loved Tag almost as much as he loved you."

Leslie gave Ava a weak smile. "This dating thing isn't easy."

Ava nodded. "You're telling me?" She shook her head. "I got lucky. BODS found Sean for me right out of the chute. I can't believe you have to sort through four men in order to come up with the right one. BODS should have narrowed it down a lot more than that."

Leslie shook her head. "I'm okay with the four-person selection that BODS came up with. I kind of like having a menu to choose from."

"I'm glad I only had the one to choose from," Ava said, wrinkling her nose.

Leslie smiled at her assistant. "I love that you're so happy with Sean. And I love that he's so good with Mica."

"Speaking of Sean and Mica…" Ava stared down at her watch. "Oh, wow. I only have a few minutes to get ready and get back home before Sean picks me up. And I have to get Mica to the babysitter." Ava's hands tightened on Leslie's arms. "We're all going to be together tonight at the rehearsal and the rehearsal dinner. Give yourself a chance with Tag. If nothing comes of it…no regrets."

Leslie smiled at her friend and assistant. "I'll keep that in mind."

Ava released Leslie's arms and spun. "I better get."

As Ava ran out of the office, Leslie called after her, "Are you bringing your dress tonight?"

"Yes, ma'am," Ava said, turning and flashing her a smile.

"They have a place for us to leave our dresses in the church overnight. I'd rather leave them there tonight than accidentally forget to bring it tomorrow. It's a long drive between Austin and Hellfire, if I have to go back to retrieve my dress."

"Good point," Ava said.

"Want me to call Fiona and remind her to bring her dress?" Leslie asked.

"That would be a good idea." Ava looped her purse over her shoulder and walked backwards toward the exit. "I'll see you tonight then. Don't forget to call Fiona."

"I won't forget. See ya there," Leslie called out.

Then Ava was out the door, leaving the office in silence.

Leslie had thirty minutes before she had to leave to reach her house, gather her things and get dressed. That gave her thirty minutes to figure out what to say in response to Joe Fox's message.

She sat at her desk then clicked her mouse to awaken the BODS system. Moments later, she had the system up and was logged into her account. She read through the message Joe had sent the night before. Then she sat with her hands on the keys.

Dear Joe

No, no, no. Was it too soon to call him dear?

Leslie erased the greeting and started over.

116

Hi Joe,

I have to admit I smile when I see your name, Joe Fox. I knew that I recognized that name from somewhere. I just couldn't put my finger on where. It took some friends of mine to figure out that it was the name of a character from the movie, You've Got Mail. I love that you chose the name of a character from that movie starring Tom Hanks and Meg Ryan. Tom Hanks is one of my favorite actors. And I love the original movie Shop Around the Corner, starring Jimmy Stewart. Some women would have been angry over the fake name being used as a cover for who you really are. I, however, understand the need for anonymity at times. Anonymity gives us a quiet place to get to know each other. You've Got Mail and Shop Around the Corner ended in a happily-ever-after for the characters. I have to believe that means you're coming into the situation with hope for a happy ending. As you can tell, I prefer to be positive. I prefer to find the joy in everything. As a good friend of mine said just recently, "Life is short, you have to grab for the joy and leave behind no regrets."

Until we meet, may your days be filled with beauty and sunshine.

Leslie

SHE STARED at the screen a moment longer, checking for typos and reading back through what she'd said. It might be corny; it might mean nothing to him. But it made her feel somehow closer to Joe Fox.

Her finger hovered over the send key for only a moment. Then she pressed it, and the message was off to Joe. She glanced at the clock, and her heart skipped several beats. She needed to get going if she was going to be on time. Tag would be at her house in thirty minutes to pick her up and she wanted to get her dress ready. It would take at least fifteen to twenty minutes to get to her house in the late afternoon Austin traffic. She grabbed her purse and ran out the office door, only stopping long enough to lock it.

Thirty minutes later, she'd called Fiona about the dress, driven across town and pulled into her driveway beside Tag's truck. Traffic had been horrible.

Tag got out of his truck, opened her SUV door for her and smiled. "You look a little stressed."

She gave him a twisted smile. "I think I hit every red light between here and the office—some of which I sat through twice." She shook her head, gathered her purse and got out.

"It's okay. We have time." Tag cupped her elbow and guided her toward her front door.

"Want me to wait in the truck?"

"Oh, no, that's not necessary," she said. "You can come in and relax. I even have a beer in the refrigerator, if you want one."

He took her keys from her, unlocked her door and opened it. Then he handed her keys back to her.

"Thanks, but I'll pass on the beer for now. I want to make sure I have a clear head for the rehearsal. From what Coop said, the wedding planner is a tough taskmaster who wants the rehearsal to go smoothly and quickly. I don't want to slow that woman down."

Leslie laughed. "I'll only be a moment. I have to gather my dress and change into something more comfortable than this suit."

She walked through the house and into her bedroom, calling out over her shoulder, "How formal do we have to be for the rehearsal?"

"I have no idea," Tag said. "All I know is that after the rehearsal, we're going to the Ugly Stick Saloon for the rehearsal dinner and to celebrate the happy couple's last night as single people."

"Well, if we're going to the Ugly Stick Saloon, I'm sure we're not going to be that formal," Leslie said.

"Right. I'm sure jeans and a T-shirt will be fine."

Leslie chuckled. "Well, maybe not quite that casual, but definitely not this suit." She left the door to her bedroom open so that she could hear Tag if he were to say something to her while she was getting her clothes ready. She riffled through her closet, looking for something appropriate to wear to a rehearsal and dinner. Finally, she selected a light blue sundress with white daisies printed on the fabric. The dress and a pair of white cowboy boots would be perfect for a night out at the Ugly Stick Saloon.

Leslie stripped out of her suit jacket and hung it

in her closet. She glanced through the door to where Tag stood in the living room with his back to her. Quickly, she shimmied out of her skirt and hung it with the suit jacket. Standing in her panties and a soft pink shell, she looked out at Tag and wondered what he'd think if he saw her standing there nearly naked. Heat coiled inside.

"Have you contacted Herman Lansing yet?" Tag asked.

As he started to turn, Leslie dove for the closet. "Yes, as a matter of fact, I did around three o'clock this afternoon. I mentioned that I'd be available Sunday. He agreed that Sunday was good for him."

"I contacted Chrissy Trent today. I asked if she was available for Sunday as well."

Standing in her closet, Leslie stripped out of the pink shell and pulled the sundress over her head. Once she had the dress smoothed down over her hips, she stepped out of the closet and smiled toward Tag. "And was she available for Sunday?"

Tag nodded. "She is. Did Herman give you a meeting place?"

Leslie turned and bent to fish her white cowboy boots out of the back of the closet.

Behind her, she heard Tag chuckling.

She straightened with her boots in hand, a frown pulling her eyebrows downward. "What's so funny?"

Tag waved a hand toward her. "You...uh..." He

shook his head and walked into the bedroom. "Turn around."

Leslie turned her back to him. "What?"

Tag tugged the hem of her dress, his knuckles brushing over her backside, sending a rush of excitement through her.

"You had your dress tucked into the back of your panties." He turned her around, a strained smile on his face. "And by the way, I like the pink lace."

Leslie's cheeks flooded with heat. If it were any other man, she would have slapped his face for such familiarity. But this was Tag. As always, he was looking out for her. "Thanks."

He grinned. "Can't have my plus-one date walking around mooning everyone tonight."

"That would be a fate worse than death," Leslie said with a crooked grin.

"Didn't bother me in the least," Tag said. "But I know you. You would have been highly embarrassed."

She nodded. "Thank you for saving me from stealing the show at the rehearsal. After all, this is Emma's night. Not my night to shine."

"Ha, ha. I love your pun. And that you have a sense of humor."

"And I love that you're always looking out for me." Leslie smiled up at Tag. "Now that you've covered my butt, we should probably get going." She slipped her feet into the boots, grabbed her bridesmaid dress, shoes and her purse and headed for the front door. How ironic that she'd been hiding in her closet to keep Tag from seeing her in her underpants, only to have her dress catch in the elastic of her panties. So, he saw her underwear anyway.

Tag held the door for her. As she passed through, a little smile slipped across his face.

Leslie frowned, wondering what he was thinking. Had he been embarrassed for her, or had he liked what he'd seen?

His arm brushed hers as she walked through the door. A shock of electricity raced up her arm and through her body, culminating low in her belly. If she lived up to her promise to Ava to keep her options open, the evening could turn out to be very interesting. The best part was that she'd be surrounded by people she knew, and no strangers.

Leslie shot a sideways glance at Tag. He wore crisply ironed blue jeans, dark brown cowboy boots, a long-sleeved, button-down white shirt and a bolo tie. Around his waist was a thick, leather belt with a shiny silver buckle. The man was handsome. There was no doubt in Leslie's mind that he could have any woman he wanted with a crook of his finger.

"You really are ready for a night at the Ugly Stick, aren't you?" she asked.

"All I need is my cowboy hat, and I'm good to go," he said. "Cowboy hat is in the back seat of my truck."

Leslie shivered in anticipation of an exciting

evening. Not so much the wedding rehearsal, but after they reached the Ugly Stick Saloon.

Tag had promised to remind her how to do the two-step. Dancing with Tag meant he would be holding her in his arms. How much more open could she be to the possibilities?

CHAPTER 8

"Okay, everyone," Marjorie Sergeant ordered, "line up like I showed you." She clapped her hands and pointed to Sean. "Sean, you and Ava are third in line of the bridesmaids and groomsmen. Please, let's get it together."

Tag gripped Leslie's elbow and eased her back a step, making room for Sean and Ava to slip between them.

"I think Ms. Marjorie has missed her calling." Sean said. "Wedding planning is just too tame for her."

"She's putting my basic training drill sergeant to shame," Tag said.

"Shh," Ava whispered. "If you don't hush, she'll give us the stink eye again."

Leslie smothered a giggle and cleared her throat. "She's just doing her job."

Tag snorted. "And that job happens to be herding cats." He liked that Leslie was having a hard time holding back her laughter. It made him feel light-hearted and happy.

Gage shot a glance over his shoulder. "You guys settle down back there. There's a beer with my name on it, waiting for me at the Ugly Stick Saloon."

"Good point," Tag said. He tipped his head toward the wedding planner. "Pay attention to Marjorie, Sean."

"At this rate, we'll be lucky to make it all the way through the ceremony tomorrow," Coop said.

"It'll be okay," Emma said. "All these guys have to do is walk down the aisle. You and I are the ones with the important lines."

"Thank goodness, all we have to do is repeat what the preacher tells us to," Coop said.

"Piece of cake," Gage said.

"Cue the music," the wedding planner called out.

The pianist played a few bars of *Friends in Low Places*.

The men all laughed.

The wedding planner glared. "I promised to get you out of here in thirty minutes. I need everyone's cooperation to make that happen."

Moose popped a salute. "Yes, ma'am." He turned to the others. "You heard the lady. Straighten up."

"Thank you." Marjorie nodded. "Now, let's get this show on the road."

The pianist played the correct music.

Moose and Jane started down the aisle, taking slow steps as instructed by the wedding planner. Gage and Fiona followed. After them, came Sean and Ava.

"It's our turn," Tag said. He meant those words in more ways than one.

Leslie tucked her hand into the crook of his elbow.

He covered it with one of his own and held on tightly.

Coop had taken his position at the front of the chapel. As the bridesmaids and the groomsmen filled in on either side, the music slowed to a stop. Everyone faced the back of the chapel as the wedding march began.

Emma appeared at the end of the aisle with her hand tucked in her oldest brother Ace's arm. She had a smile on her face that could have eclipsed the sun. Tag's heart squeezed hard in his chest. How he wished he could see Leslie standing at the end of the aisle smiling just as brightly, walking toward him. He glanced across the aisle at Leslie.

Her gaze captured his for a long, intense moment.

"Can we speed this up?" Emma said. "I hear the beer calling me from the Ugly Stick Saloon."

Coop grinned. "That's my girl."

The piano player sped up the wedding march

until Emma was skipping down the aisle with her brother. They arrived laughing.

The wedding planner pointed to the exact spot where Emma and Coop should stand.

The preacher gave a brief version of what their vows would be like. "Coop, do you?"

Coop nodded.

The preacher turned to Emma. "Emma, do you?"

Emma nodded.

The preacher smiled. "I now pronounce you."

Coop grinned. "This is the part where I get to kiss the bride." He gathered her into his arms and laid a kiss on her that was loud and long.

"Hey, save some for tomorrow," Sean said.

Emma came up laughing. "Oh, if only it were this short tomorrow."

"We can make that happen." The preacher winked. "This is it for me. The rest is up to you."

Coop looked up at his friends. "Who's ready for a beer?"

"Hold on a minute," the wedding planner said. "We still need to practice getting out of the church."

"How hard can that be?" Coop asked.

"Easy. As long as you listen to what I say." Marjorie pointed at the bride and groom. "You two, go."

Emma's eyes widened. "Are we done after this?"

The wedding planner nodded. "You're free to go.

Just be here at least an hour early for the wedding tomorrow."

"We'll be here," Coop said. He faced his friends. "Last one to the Ugly Stick buys the first round."

Emma grabbed Coop's hand. "Let's go."

The bride and groom raced down the aisle and out of the church.

The wedding planner tipped her head. "Moose and Jane, you're up next."

Moose and Jane came together at the middle, grasped hands and ran down the aisle, laughing.

As soon as the couple passed the wedding planner, she nodded to the next couple. "Sean and Ava, you're next."

When Sean and Ava came together, he scooped her off the ground and carried her through the church.

Tag could hear her laughter all the way out of the building.

"Tag and Leslie," Marjorie called out.

A wicked grin slid across Tag's face. He stalked toward Leslie.

Leslie approached him cautiously. "What are you up to?"

"This." He bent and flung her over his shoulder in a fireman's carry and ran down the aisle and out into the open.

"Taggert...Bronson...put me down," she cried.

Tag didn't put her down until he reached his

truck outside the church. He let her slide down his body until her feet touched the ground. "How was that for making a fast getaway?"

Leslie laughed breathlessly, pressed a hand to her belly and sucked in a deep breath. "Please, tell me you're not going to do that tomorrow."

"What? You don't like being carried out like a caveman's woman?" He grinned and held up his hand. "I swear on a stack of bibles I won't do that tomorrow."

Leslie stared at him with narrowed eyes. "How can I trust you not to do something equally silly?"

His grin broadened. "You can't trust me. But I promise not to hurt you."

Leslie shook her head. "Weddings are supposed to be a serious event."

Tag nodded. "Yes, they should be serious events. And they should be fun. After all, a wedding is a celebration of happiness shared by two people in love." He opened the truck door and handed Leslie up into the passenger seat.

"True," she said. "Just remember that bridesmaid dresses aren't made for manhandling." Though she wore a stern expression, her lips twitched.

"I'll try to keep that in mind." Tag grinned broadly, rounded the truck, climbed into the driver's seat and started the engine. He pulled out onto the highway. The race was on to get to the Ugly Stick Saloon before the last man arrived.

Tag broke a few speed limits and ran a couple stop signs between the chapel and the saloon. He arrived in the parking lot two seconds before Gage and Fiona. Slamming the shift into park, he leaped down from his seat and ran around the side to help Leslie down. He grabbed her hand and ran for the saloon, arriving at the same time as Gage and Fiona, laughing.

Tag opened the door and held it for Leslie and Fiona. Gage dove through before Tag could stop him. Tag entered the saloon last, shaking his head.

"Guess who's buying the beer tonight?" Sean said.

Tag's mouth twisted into a wry grin. It wasn't like he couldn't afford to buy the first round of beer. And he really didn't mind. His friends were like his brothers. They meant the world to him. "All right, the first round is on me."

Tag walked to the bar and slapped his credit card on the surface. "What can I get you, Leslie?"

"I'll have a draft beer," she said.

Once he had their beer mugs in hand, Tag led Leslie to the large table where the bride, groom, bridesmaids and groomsmen had gathered.

They had reserved the entire saloon for the dinner, setting aside two hours just for them. After that, the saloon would open to all patrons. Someone had loaded the juke box with coins, and music was playing.

They ate their meal of barbeque brisket, potato salad and beans, talking and laughing throughout.

When the food was cleared away and drinks replenished, Sean raised his beer mug. "I'd like to propose a toast."

"Who are we toasting?" Coop asked.

"To Marjorie," Sean said, nodding toward the wedding planner who sat with Emma's brothers alongside the preacher. "Best drill sergeant ever. She got us to our beer on time."

Everyone lifted their drinks. "To Marjorie!"

Tag grinned and downed a deep swallow of his beer.

Coop raised his mug. "I'd like to propose a toast."

Emma frowned. "You're not supposed to propose toasts. You're the groom."

Coop grinned. "I'd like to propose that we don't propose anymore toasts for the evening."

Everyone raised their drinks. "Here! Here!"

"This might be the last time I get to dance with a single woman. I'm going to take full advantage of this opportunity. My future wife has a jealous streak a mile wide." Coop winked, downed a swallow of his beer, set his mug on the table, grabbed Emma's hand and dragged her out onto the dance floor.

Emma laughed as Coop swung her into his arms.

Leslie set her drink on the table and glanced across at Tag. "Aren't you going to ask me to dance?"

Tag nodded. "I was just about to do that."

"Good. I want to see just how good you are at the two-step." Leslie took his hand and led him out onto the floor.

Tag twirled her into his arms and danced her around the floor in a lively two-step. He was pleased at how easily she kept up with him.

"Randy didn't like to dance," Leslie said. "I'm glad you do."

Before he'd lost Leslie to Randy, Tag had not liked dancing either. He'd made it his business to figure out what Leslie liked and didn't like. He hadn't set out consciously to learn to dance because of her. He told himself that many women liked to dance, and even more men didn't. If he planned on reentering the dating scene, and if he wanted to find a woman like Leslie, he had to learn to dance.

The song came to a close, immediately followed by the Cotton-Eyed Joe.

"Are you game for this one?" Tag asked.

Leslie nodded. "I'm game, if you are."

"Let's do this."

Around and around, they danced to the Cotton-Eyed Joe, along with everyone else. As the song progressed, the music sped up until they were kicking and shuffling as fast as they could to keep up. The song came to a breathless end. Everyone on the dance floor stopped, laughed and held onto their aching sides.

The next song was slow and easy. The kind of

song made for belly rubbing and belt buckle polishing. Tag held Leslie's hands in his and stared down into her eyes. "Are you up for one more?"

She chuckled. "As long as all I have to do is stand here and sway, I'm good for another."

Tag pulled her close. "We can sway. No pressure. No fancy dance moves." He rested his lips near her temple and inhaled a deep breath. "Your hair smells like honeysuckle in the summertime."

Leslie chuckled. "I hope that's a compliment, and that you're not allergic to honeysuckle."

"Trust me, it was a compliment. I love the scent of honeysuckle," he said and gathered her closer.

As promised, he stood in one place swaying back and forth with Leslie in his arms. He couldn't think of any place he'd rather be. When the song came to an end, he pressed a kiss to her temple. Then he took her elbow and guided her back to the table where the others had taken their seats.

"Can I get you another beer?" he asked.

Leslie nodded.

Tag didn't wait for the waitress to come take their order. He walked toward the bar and leaned his foot on the rail. He needed a moment or two away from Leslie. The more he was with her, the more he wanted to be with her. He wanted to hold her close and kiss her until they both needed a long, steadying breath.

He sighed.

Tag wasn't sure she was ready for him to make his move.

Leslie sat beside Ava at the table, surrounded by their friends. She'd never felt so included as she did at that moment. At the same time, she felt like she didn't quite fit in. Everyone else at the table was paired off. Everyone except her and Tag.

Ava leaned toward her. "I noticed you and Tag getting pretty cozy out there on the dance floor."

Leslie glanced in Tag's direction. She couldn't deny the man was handsome. Nor could she deny that she was attracted. At that moment, Tag smiled at one of the waitresses.

Leslie's heart pinched hard in her chest. How could she be jealous of a waitress, when she had no ties to Tag? He didn't belong to her, and she didn't belong to him. At that moment, Leslie found herself wishing she did belong to Tag. How weird would that be? Tag was her husband's best friend.

"Earth to Leslie," Ava said.

Leslie shook her head and turned to Ava. "Sorry, did you say something?"

Ava rolled her eyes. "Why are you bothering to date other men?"

Leslie frowned. "What do you mean?"

"You don't need to date other men." Ava tipped

her head. "Everything you need in a man is right in front of you."

Leslie glanced at her hands instead of the man at the bar. "Ava, I told you. Tag is my friend. I don't want to screw up that friendship."

"How are you going to screw up your friendship with Tag?"

"He's been with me every step of the way since my husband's death," Leslie said. "If we throw in a romantic element between us, and it doesn't work out, then what? That friendship will be compromised."

Ava took Leslie's hands in hers. "Sometimes, you gotta take a risk." Ava looked toward Tag. "Do you find him attractive at all?"

Heat rose up Leslie's neck into her cheeks. "Of course, I do."

Ava laughed. "There's no 'of course' about it. I don't find him attractive...well, as attractive as I find Sean. He is an attractive man. He just doesn't appeal to me like my Sean does."

Leslie sighed. "Yes, I find him attractive."

"Then why don't you go for him?" Ava asked.

Leslie shrugged. "I don't know. Maybe I'm not ready. Maybe he's too good for me."

Her friend snorted. "You're both good people. I believe you could make each other happy. I believe he could be your future baby daddy." Ava looked at her. "Have you thought about that?"

Leslie watched as Tag came back across the floor, carrying two mugs of beer. Yes, she'd thought of him as the father of her children. And, immediately, she'd felt guilty. She had the sperm from her dead husband stored in a bank. "Randy and I had planned on having children. I still have the sperm we saved back when we discovered he was dying. What am I supposed to do? Just ignore them?"

"It's just sperm. Frozen sperm, at that," Ava reminded her.

"It's more than that." Leslie's gaze still on Tag, she continued, "It's like there are babies waiting at that sperm bank. Babies who are relying on me to realize the dream Randy and I had for children."

"If you have those children," Ava said, "you run the risk of complicating any other relationship you hope to have with another man. After all, it's hard for a man to accept the children of another man." Ava added quickly, "However, since Tag was a close friend of Randy's, wouldn't he be more accepting of Randy's children?"

Leslie didn't get the chance to answer that question, but Ava's observation rolled around in her mind. How would Tag feel about raising Randy's children? Was it fair of her to ask Tag to raise Randy's children?

Tag arrived at the table and set the two beers down in front of her. "You must be thinking some very heavy thoughts," he said.

"Why do you say that?" Leslie asked.

He brushed a thumb across her forehead. "You're frowning."

She focused on smoothing her brow. "Is that better?"

"It's a start." He held out his hand. "Ready to dance again?"

Emma grabbed Coop and dragged him toward the floor. Sean plucked Ava from her chair and joined them. Moose and Jane were next. Gage and Fiona followed. Even Emma's brothers found waitresses to dance with. Everyone hurried to the dance floor for a line dance.

She glanced up at Tag, feeling vulnerable and overwhelmed. "I don't know this dance."

He smiled. "It's the Cupid Shuffle. It's easy. I'll help you."

"I don't know," she said, her thoughts roiling with everything she and Ava had discussed.

He held her hand tight in his, refusing to let her backslide into herself. "Come on, darlin'. One more dance."

When he put it that way, how could she resist?

She couldn't. Leslie let him pull her to her feet and out onto the dance floor.

Within moments, she was holding his hand, laughing and dancing along with the others. For a brief time, she could forget everything and enjoy the few minutes she spent with Tag.

When the song was over, she tugged his hand. "Take me home, please."

His brow furrowed. "Are you feeling all right?"

No. "Yes. I'm just tired, and tomorrow will be a long day."

He nodded. "Let's say our goodbyes and hit the road."

After hugging Emma and Coop, and waving at the rest of the group, Leslie and Tag took their leave and left the saloon, pushing through the crowd waiting outside for the doors to open to the public.

Leslie was glad they were leaving before the saloon was overrun by the usual Friday night crowd. She had a lot to think about, and a crowded room would only make it harder.

They'd been in the truck driving toward Austin for ten minutes before either one of them spoke.

Tag broke the silence with, "The wedding will be nice tomorrow. Coop and Emma make a great couple."

"Emma deserves all the happiness," Leslie agreed. "I'm honored to be a part of it."

"Your wedding to Randy was much smaller," Tag noted.

"We didn't know a lot of people at the time. We had those who were important to us there." She smiled across at him. "You were there."

He nodded. "I'm happy for Coop and Emma, but I think I'd want a different kind of wedding."

"Yeah?" She studied him from her side of the cab. "What would you do differently?"

"I'd have it at my ranch, surrounded by family and friends. A quick ceremony to tie the knot, and then a barbeque and music. No fuss. Not a lot of work."

Leslie laughed. "Even that would be a lot of work. You'd want to have a photographer present to take photos of you and your bride. Someone would have to contract a DJ or band for your music. The barbeque wouldn't happen on its own. Someone would have to cater to bring it in and clean up afterward. And you'd have to schedule a preacher, JP or someone certified to perform the ceremony."

Tag's lips twisted. "Wow. And I thought it would be simpler." He shook his head. "I guess that's why Coop and Emma hired Marjorie."

"I talked with Emma when she started planning the wedding. That's when we found Marjorie." Leslie smiled. "She's good."

"I guess I'd have to do that as well. I wouldn't expect my bride to be stuck with all the planning."

"Unless she wants to do it," Leslie murmured, thinking about the other dates BODS had matched him with. What if one of them was the future Mrs. Bronson?

Her chest tightened. She wanted Tag to be happy with whomever he chose as his bride. Though she wasn't sure she was ready for such a big commitment for herself, in the back of her mind, her

subconscious was waving her hand, saying, *Pick me!*
Pick me!

They dropped into silence again, remaining there
until they arrived at her house in Austin. Leslie didn't
wait for Tag to open the door for her. She pushed it
open and dropped down out of truck. By that time, Tag
had rounded the front and held out his hand to her.

She took it and let him hold it all the way up to
the door. It felt right she didn't let go, even when she
handed him the key to her door. She held onto his
free hand as he unlocked her front door.

Holding his hand felt so right that she didn't want
to let go. When Tag leaned down to kiss her cheek,
Leslie turned her face at the last second.

Their lips met.

She leaned into him, wanting to know what it felt
like to be kissed thoroughly by this man, to be held in
his arms and pressed up against his body.

His hands swept down her back and pulled her
close, their hips touching, the hard evidence of his
desire nudging her belly.

She'd thought kissing Tag would feel weird,
somehow a betrayal of her love for Randy. But it
didn't feel that way at all. It felt good, hot and addic-
tive. She couldn't get enough.

Leslie wrapped her arms around his neck and
deepened the kiss, opening to him.

Tag's tongue slipped past her teeth to sweep the

length of hers, caressing hers in long, sensuous thrusts.

What had started as curiosity had morphed into frenetic lust that couldn't be satisfied while they were on her front porch and fully dressed. She wanted to be naked with this man.

That thought entering her head served as a splash of ice water on her senses. She pulled free, her heart beating hard, her breathing ragged. "I'm sorry. I shouldn't have done that."

Tag reached for her. "Leslie—"

"No, it was my fault." She shook her head. "I…I… have to go." She dove past him into her house, slamming the door behind her.

She leaned against it, twisting the lock, without looking back. Not so much to keep him out, but to keep her from opening the door and flinging herself into his arms.

What had she done?

A knock sounded. "Leslie. Open the door," Tag called out softly.

She shook her head. "No," she whispered.

"Leslie, I'm not sorry that happened," Tag called out. "I've wanted to kiss you all night long."

Tears filled her eyes and rolled down her cheeks. Her thoughts were a mess of what she wanted, what she'd had and how the hell she could unravel the two to make a future for herself.

"I'll pick you up tomorrow," Tag said. "And, Leslie, everything is going to be okay."

"How can it be?" she murmured.

She heard his truck door slam and the engine start. When she was sure he'd gone, she left the door and walked through the house she'd shared with Randy, touching the photographs of the two of them together, staring at the one of all three of them. Finally, she entered her bedroom, toed off her cowboy boots, pulled one of Randy's old flannel shirts from the closet and wrapped it around her shoulders.

He wasn't there to tell her everything would be all right. Tag was doing that now. He wasn't there to tell her that it was okay to kiss Tag. She had to come to grips with that on her own.

All she knew at that moment was that she missed Randy and hadn't wanted to quit kissing Tag.

Man, was she messed up.

CHAPTER 9

Tag had headed to his penthouse apartment in downtown Austin after dropping off Leslie at her house. He was so wound up from her kiss, he couldn't begin to settle down and sleep. Instead, he'd poured himself a whiskey and sat in his recliner, staring at a photo of himself, Leslie and Randy.

"Randy, if you didn't want me to have her, you shouldn't have left us so soon." Tag tipped his glass, swallowing a long draught of the clear amber liquid. His gaze shifted to Leslie, with her sandy-blond hair, gray eyes and laughing smile. She was everything he needed and more. She made him want to be a better person.

He wanted to be with her, to take care of her and make her happy. She deserved all the happiness in the world. Which raised the question: *Can I make her happy?*

Was he selfish to think he was the one for her, and that they should make a life together?

Leslie had picked Randy. If she chose to be with Tag, he would always be her second choice. Would that be good enough for her? Would that be enough for him?

He drank another swallow of whiskey and stared into a fireplace he rarely used.

She'd kissed him tonight.

And run.

What did that mean?

Had he scared her off because of his whole-hearted response?

Tag buried his head in his hands.

Had he spooked her?

What happened to his plan to take it slowly? He raised his head and pushed back his shoulders. He had to get back on track, back to the slow, steady advance on her senses. If that meant backing off, so be it. He was in this pursuit for the long haul.

But if, at any time, Leslie showed signs of withdrawal, discomfort and anything else that indicated she wasn't that into him, he'd step away.

He downed the last of his drink, rose, stripped and stepped into the shower to cool off. Every time he thought of Leslie, he burned with desire. And after their kiss, he knew the fire would continue long into the night.

He had to get his lust under control or risk losing

her forever. It would be difficult to keep his feelings to himself, but Leslie Lamb was worth the effort.

Tag showered and went to bed. The cool spray did little to douse the flames burning inside. He lay naked on the sheets, staring up at the high ceilings, wishing he already had her in bed beside him.

If he played his cards right, and made her fall in love with him, his wish would come true.

He groaned, turned on his side and punched his pillow.

Playing his cards right was a big *if*.

He lay for a long time, thinking about calling her. After she'd run into her house, she probably didn't want to talk to him. He could log on to his computer and strike up an email conversation with her as his alter-ago Joe. Part of him thought any contact was better than none. What if she fell in love with Joe? Would she be disappointed when she discovered Joe was him?

Tag flopped onto his back again and shoved a hand through his hair, second-guessing his second identity on BODS. What had he been thinking? She might think he'd been leading her on and stop trusting her.

He sat up, reached for the phone and dialed her number.

After five rings, he ended the call without leaving a message.

What would he say? *I'm sorry I kissed you back?* Oh,

hell no. He wasn't the least bit sorry. For him, the kiss had been everything he'd hoped for and so much more. He'd felt the electricity and the connection from where their lips touched all the way to the tips of his toes. Since he'd realized he loved her, he'd dreamed of kissing her, wondering what it would be like. Would he like it? Would she?

Well, he knew now. He loved it and wanted to do it again and again.

AFTER HITTING the snooze on her alarm clock five times, Leslie finally woke. Sleep hadn't come easy the night before. Kissing Tag seemed to have shaken everything loose inside her. She hadn't been able to pull herself together before she'd laid in her bed to sleep.

Not once during that kiss had she thought of Randy. The kiss had been all Tag and her. No one else existed in that moment. God, she wanted to do it all over again.

All night long, she lay alone in her bed, wishing Tag was lying beside her. She hadn't gone to sleep until well after three in the morning. Thus, the rounds of slamming her hand on the snooze button.

She flung aside the comforter and swung her legs out of the bed, her first thoughts of Tag, wondering how he had slept the night before. Had he stayed awake all night, thinking about kissing her?

Leslie padded to the bathroom in her bare feet and stared into the mirror at the dark circles beneath her eyes. She splashed water on her face, hoping the coolness would help to revive her.

As she walked back through the bedroom, she spied her laptop on the nightstand. She picked it up and carried it into the kitchen. After getting the coffeemaker going, she popped a slice of bread into the toaster and sat at the table. Opening her laptop, she checked her emails.

Thankfully, she didn't have any from clients complaining that the BODS system was down. She logged onto her own account where she found a message from Herman Lansing, aka Bachelor Number Two. And nothing from Joe Fox.

With less enthusiasm than she had for a visit to the dentist, she opened the message from Herman.

Ms. Lamb,

I hope to make our date an adventure. Let's meet at Enchanted Rock. Wear hiking shoes. See you there on Sunday at 10:00 am.

Herman

Leslie sighed. Another date.

She wished she hadn't signed up on BODS. And she didn't want to go to Enchanted Rock, out in the middle of nowhere, by herself with a stranger. She needed to call Tag but couldn't bring herself to do it. Not after she'd kissed him and run the night before.

Her phone rang, saving her from making that

decision. The caller ID indicated it was Tag. She pressed the talk button, her heart hammering against her ribs.

"Good morning, sunshine," Tag's voice came through, sending a rush of heat through her body.

"Hi," she said, sounding breathless. She swallowed hard, squared her shoulders and started over. "Good morning, Tag." She cringed at how formal that sounded to her own ears. "I hope you slept well."

"Like a baby," he said, so cheerful she wanted to throw something at him.

"Me, too," she lied. "I had an email from my second candidate. He wants to meet at Enchanted Rock, Sunday at 10:00 am. I'm supposed to bring hiking shoes."

"Sounds like fun. I'll let Chrissy know to bring something to hike in. We'll be there at 10:00 as well." He paused. "Are you ready for today?"

No. She wasn't. Facing him after that kiss...she wasn't ready. "Absolutely. I can't wait."

"Good. I'll be by to pick you up in an hour. I understand Emma wanted her bridesmaids there three hours early. I can't imagine how it takes three hours to get dressed for a wedding."

Leslie forced a laugh, trying for lighthearted when she was more *down*hearted. "She has a couple of cosmetologists coming in to do hair and makeup for her and the bridesmaids."

"Meanwhile, I'll be in charge of keeping the

groom sober and making sure he gets to the front of the chapel on time." He sighed.

"How hard can that be?" she asked.

Tag chuckled. "You don't know the guys when they get bored."

"I believe the groom's room is equipped with a rather large television screen. Surely, you'll find a game playing," Leslie said, feeling a little less self-conscious after talking nonsense with Tag. He always made her feel better, even when she was confused. If he could act as though the kiss never happened, so could she.

Her chest tightened. At least, she hoped she could. Frankly, the kiss had rocked her world in a way she hadn't thought possible. The resulting desire and longing warred with guilt concerning her dead husband.

As Ava had mentioned, four years was long enough to grieve for someone you loved. Moving on didn't mean she'd ever forget Randy. He would always be a part of her, even if she found someone else to love. She had enough love in her heart to love again.

But was the love for Tag?

Her breath caught and held in her throat. Up until that moment, she hadn't paired Tag with the "L" word. Could she be in love with Tag? Or was she clinging to him because he was someone familiar? Someone who made her feel safe? After all, dating strangers was hard and scary. Especially when they wanted to take you out into the wilderness hiking. Anything could happen. She was glad Tag would be there…just in case she was dating a serial killer. Not to mention the stress of having to make conversation with someone she might have nothing in common with.

But BODS had matched her with Herman. Surely, they'd have a lot in common. After meeting Otis, she was beginning to think she should have narrowed her preferences a little more. Otis was very nice but into things she wasn't all that interested in.

Leslie dressed in comfortable jeans, a soft white, short-sleeve shirt and ballet flats, knowing that once she reached the wedding venue, she'd strip down to her panties and strapless bra and put on the silk robe Emma had gifted to all of her bridesmaids. Her long gown and shoes were waiting for her there. All she had to do was show up sans makeup. The beauticians would be there for hair and makeup.

Normally, she wouldn't be at all self-conscious in front of Tag. He'd seen her without makeup and her hair pulled back in a ponytail more times than she could count. He'd come over often when Randy was alive to watch the Aggies football games and grill steaks.

Something about the kiss the night before set Leslie on edge. She felt like she needed to look her best around him.

For heaven's sake, it was Tag. Her best friend.

Her potential lover...

That thought hit her square in the gut. The man who'd been her friend since forever. And she was thinking about getting naked with him and...and...

She pressed a hand to her belly, her core so hot she might have to take a cold shower before Tag arrived to collect her for the wedding.

Too keyed up to relax, she put on her athletic shoes and went for a walk around the neighborhood. After a mile, she'd calmed enough to return to her house.

Tag arrived shortly afterward.

Leslie had been watching through the window and didn't wait for him to come to the door. As soon as he pulled into the driveway, she left her house, locked the door and hurried toward his truck.

He saw her coming and got out to open her door. "Hey," he said, a crooked smile on his lips.

"Hey." Leslie ducked her head and climbed in, careful not to touch him, afraid the sparks would set off an inferno inside her. She had a wedding to get through. Now wasn't the time to get all hot and steamy about her best friend.

Once she was in her seat, Tag closed the door, rounded the front of the truck and climbed into the driver's seat. He sat for a minute, hesitating before starting the engine.

Leslie clenched her hands in her lap.

Please, don't say anything, just drive.

Then he glanced at her. "Look, Leslie, about last night—"

"Don't." She raised her hand. "Please. Let's not discuss last night. Today is Emma and Coop's wedding. I want to focus on them."

He opened his mouth as if to say more. A moment later, he shut it and nodded. "Okay." He started the engine, backed out of her driveway and headed for the little chapel in Hellfire where the wedding would take place.

Leslie sat silent, staring out the front windshield, afraid that if Tag spoke to her, she'd blurt out something she wasn't ready to say. She felt as if she sat on pins and needles, her entire being on edge and ready to erupt into...something. What, she wasn't sure. But it all had to do with Tag...and that kiss.

SEVERAL TIMES along the drive out to the wedding venue, Tag nearly pulled to the side of the road to have it out with Leslie. He was past ready to declare his feelings and get them out into the open. He'd held back for so long he didn't think he could do it for much longer.

However, the longer she sat on her side of the truck without saying a word, the harder it became to strike up a conversation, especially when all he wanted to say was, *I love you, dammit!*

When they arrived at the wedding venue, Tag parked in the shade of an oak tree. Before he could get out of the truck, Leslie shoved open her door and slid out.

She disappeared into the manor house where the ladies would prepare for the wedding. The men would be in the carriage house on the other side of the chapel.

Tag wanted to go after her, grab her arm and force her to look at him. But she was gone before he could. He grabbed the tux hanging in the back seat and headed for the carriage house.

Coop, Gage, Moose and Sean were inside, along with Emma's brothers Ace, Dillon, Brand and Colton. They were arguing over the remote control in Coop's hand.

The poor man was still dressed in his jeans and a T-shirt, his hair standing on end, and his eyes a little wild.

"About time you showed up, Tag," Sean said. "We were just having a friendly little discussion about what game to watch on the big screen television."

Tag's brow wrinkled. "What discussion? The Aggies are playing. End of discussion."

"So are the Longhorns," Ace said. "The Aggies don't know what a football is, much less how to play."

Coop shook his head. "I didn't know I was marrying into a family of Longhorns. This could be a deal-breaker."

"Perhaps we should get Emma over here to settle this," Colton said. "Does she know you'd rather watch an Aggies game over a Longhorn game?"

Coop gave him a wry grin. "I don't think the subject ever came up. But now that it has…" He glanced toward the door. "I'm not sure we can be married if that's the way the ball bounces." Coop started for the door. "Maybe we need to call this whole thing off."

Ace, Brand, Colton and Dillon lined up in front of the door, arms crossed over their chests.

Coop cocked an eyebrow. "What? You won't let me call it off over a football game?"

All four of Emma's brothers shook their heads as one, their jaws firm, eyes narrowed.

"You aren't walking out on our little sister," Ace said. "She's had her heart broken once. It's not going to happen again."

"Then we're watching the Aggies game while we wait…?" Coop said, holding up the remote.

"We don't have to argue about this when we can accommodate both games on this set." Tag grabbed the remote from him, hit the menu button and selected the option to split the screen. He brought up both games and set the remote on the mantel. "We can watch both while we get ready for the wedding." He looked at the all eight men and grinned. "Are you happy now? The wedding's still on, and Coop isn't going to be lynched."

"I guess we can watch it this way," Coop said grudgingly. "But you're going to have to show me how to do that on my home screen. I don't want to get a divorce over what football game we'll watch."

"You'll watch whatever Emma wants you to watch." Moose pounded Coop on the back. "A happy wife makes a happy life."

"That's right, Coop. You're getting married, today," Gage said. "The first of us to walk down the aisle. How does it feel to be standing on the cusp of bachelorhood, about to launch into married life?"

Coop drew in a deep breath and patted his chest. "I thought I'd be sad to say goodbye to my single days." He shook his head and grinned. "But I'm not. I'm marrying the best girl in the world." His grin twisted. "Well, with the exception of being a Longhorn fan. But nobody's perfect."

"You're lucky we'll let you slide on that one," Brand said. "If our sister wasn't so darned happy, we might have had to run you out of town."

Gage popped the top on a bottle of beer and handed it to Coop. "Make that one last. It's the only one you're getting until you say I do."

"Can't wait until you guys go through this. I promise, I'll make you just as miserable," Coop said and took a slow swallow of his beer, closing his eyes as the cool liquid went down his throat. He opened his eyes, a frown denting his forehead. "Speaking of which, when are you getting hitched, Moose, Sean,

Gage? You might as well do it on the same day and get 'er done."

"No way," Moose said. "I want Jane coming down that aisle all by herself. We'll set a date soon. I don't want to wait too long. She might change her mind." Moose sighed. "I can't believe she fell for me."

"You're not the only one who can't believe it," Sean said, elbowing the big ex-football player in the side.

"What about you, Sean?" Moose asked. "When are you, Ava and Mica gonna make it legal?"

"The sooner the better. I told Ava I'd fly her and Mica to Vegas and get it done."

"Better charter an entire plane," Tag said. "You're not getting married without the rest of us."

"As for us, Fiona's about got horseback riding mastered." Moose grinned. "She said she'd schedule our wedding as soon as she could get married on horseback."

Tag chuckled. "That should be an interesting wedding." He popped the top off another bottle of beer.

"She knows how much I love riding and wants us to ride off into the sunset." Gage grinned. "I like the idea. I just wonder if the horses will behave through an entire ceremony."

"Which leaves the rest of you," Coop said, his gaze moving from Tag to Emma's four brothers. "Tag, at least, is in the process of finding Mrs. Right. What about the rest of you?"

Ace held up his hands. "I don't need help finding a woman."

"Neither do I," Brand said.

Colton shrugged. "I don't know. That match-making program that got you guys hooked up with your gals has me thinkin'."

"Me, too," Dillon said. "Can't imagine living with you boneheads for the rest of my life."

"Yeah," Colton said. "I would kinda like to have a wife to come home to, instead of a bunch of guys who smell like something the cat dragged in."

Tag grinned. "I'll have Leslie schedule you guys to sign up on her dating service. You won't regret it."

"Speaking of regrets," Coop said. "What's happening with you and your dates, Tag? Any luck?"

Tag nodded. "I'm working on it. I was matched with three lovely ladies. I've been on one date already. I see the second lady tomorrow."

"I hear the first one was all into Comic Con and Dr. Who," Sean said. He shook his head. "I'm not picturing you at one of those conventions."

Tag grinned. "We went to one."

His eyebrows rose. "And you liked it?"

He liked being with Leslie. "It was fun." With Leslie.

"And when you two get married, we're all going to

be in costume?" Sean laughed. "I call dibs on Iron Man."

"I'll come as Hulk," Moose said.

"I call Thor," Coop said.

Tag shook his head. "I'm not getting married at a comic book convention. And I'm not marrying Twyla."

"That certain about your first match?" Gage asked.

Tag nodded. "Absolutely. She's not the one for me."

"Maybe Bachelorette Number Two will be more to your liking," Sean said. "You better get with the picture. The rest of us are meeting the goals we set for ourselves. You're the last holdout."

"I'm working on it," Tag said. "I hope to have good news soon."

Coop draped an arm over Tag's shoulder. "I'm glad to hear it. I'd like to think we'll have kids around the same time so they can grow up together."

"That's right," Moose said. "Jane wants a bunch."

"So does Fiona," Gage said.

"And Ava wants a brother or sister for Mica," Sean said.

"Don't worry. I've got a plan," Tag said. And he prayed it worked out. This time next year, he hoped to be married and for them to be well on their way to having those kids everyone was talking about.

They watched the last half of the games, cheering

on the Longhorns and the Aggies. Both teams won, leaving all nine men happy.

Tag glanced at his watch. They had thirty minutes until the wedding planner would round them up and herd them over to the chapel. "Okay, guys, the fun's over. It's time to get serious. We've got to get Coop to the church on time."

They hurried into their suits, pinned on boutonnieres and combed their hair. Tag went down the line, inspecting all the men.

They all looked amazing.

Emma's brothers left to usher guests into the chapel, leaving the five men of the Billionaires Anonymous Club to await their cue.

"Coop," Tag said. "I wish you all the love and happiness you and Emma deserve." He hugged his friend. "Love you, man."

"Thanks," Coop said. "It'll be your turn soon."

Tag was counting on it. He wished he was Coop and Leslie was Emma, and they were the ones getting married that day.

After Sean, Moose and Gage hugged Coop, they opened the door to find Marjorie standing there with her hand raised to knock. "Ready?" she asked.

Coop nodded. "Ready. Lead the way."

The men filed out of the carriage house and crossed the lawn to the chapel.

Coop entered and went to the front of the chapel to wait for his bride.

The bridesmaids came out of the manor house and lined up next to their respective groomsmen.

Tag smiled down at Leslie. She was stunning in a deep red gown, her sandy blond hair pulled back on one side, the other swinging free, cupping her chin. She was beautiful, and he couldn't take his eyes off her.

She kept her head down, her eyes on the small bouquet of white roses in her hands.

The preacher did his job, Coop and Emma said their vows and he pronounced them husband and wife.

"You may kiss your bride," the minister said.

Coop yelled, "Yeehaw!", grabbed Emma and kissed her, then kissed her some more, dipping her low in his arms.

Everyone in the church clapped.

Tag's gaze left the couple and crossed the aisle to Leslie. She was watching Coop and Emma kiss, her eyes filled with tears. Then she turned to him, her gaze colliding with his.

Tears slid down her cheeks. She wiped at the them and squared her shoulders, lifting her chin.

Coop and Emma turned to the congregation and smiled.

Leslie helped the bridesmaids straighten Emma's train as she swept down the aisle and out of the church where the photographer was waiting to take pictures of the bride and groom.

As Marjorie had choreographed, each couple met at the middle and left the church together.

When Tag met Leslie at the center, he held out his arm to her.

She slipped her hand into the crook of his elbow. He covered hers with his and led her out into the late afternoon sunshine.

After another thirty minutes of photographs, they were free to go to the reception at the Ugly Stick Saloon.

Still, Leslie hadn't said more than two words to Tag.

He was getting worried that he'd blown his chance with her. They made the short trip from Hellfire to the Ugly Stick Saloon on the county line in complete and strained silence. Tag wasn't sure how to cut through the thick air in the cab and get Leslie to talk about what she was feeling.

Thankfully, they arrived at the Ugly Stick Saloon along with the rest of the wedding party. The celebration was in full swing. They had the saloon for the next three hours, with a band on the stage and the waitresses serving champagne, whiskey and beer as fast as they could.

The leader of the band announced the bride and groom's first dance.

Emma and Coop took the floor in their wedding togs, moving to a waltz. Tag was proud of Coop, who'd taken lessons just to make Emma look good on the dance floor. He did beautifully.

After their dance, all the other couples joined them.

Angry with himself for going off the plan the night before, and the fact Leslie wasn't talking to him, Tag did the only thing he could think of. He took Leslie's hand and led her out onto the dance floor. When he pulled her into his arms, he whispered in her ear, "You don't have to talk to dance."

Finally, she looked up, met his gaze and slid into his arms.

Tag held her so close their hips moved as one to the sweet, slow beat of a tender love song. The more they swayed together, the more she relaxed against him, her hands resting on the lapels of his suit, her fingers curling into the fabric.

Long after the music ended, they continued to sway, lost in a world where it was just him and Leslie.

The band leader cleared his throat, and everyone laughed.

Tag looked up to see that they were the only couple remaining on the dance floor, and the bride stood to the side, holding her bouquet.

"If the couple still dancing could take a break," the band leader said, "the bride would like to give the single ladies a chance at happiness. That's right—it's time to throw the bouquet. Single ladies, please line up on the dance floor.

Tag's arms dropped to his sides, and he moved toward the table where the men congregated.

He didn't like letting go of Leslie. If he wasn't mistaken, they'd had a moment on that dance floor, and he wasn't sure he'd get it back.

He didn't have a choice. The other women circled Leslie, blocking her escape. As he watched, they maneuvered her away from him and closer to Emma.

Tag found himself hoping Leslie would be the lucky one who caught the bouquet. He needed all the help he could get to make her see that getting married again was not only in the cards, it was fate.

CHAPTER 10

LESLIE STARTED to follow Tag from the floor, but was headed off by Ava, Fiona and Jane.

"Oh, no, you don't," Ava said. "You're the only one of us single ladies who isn't engaged. You're going to catch that bouquet if it's the last thing you do tonight."

Leslie's brow furrowed. "It's not fair to other single ladies for me to be out there. I've been married before."

"Are you married now?" Fiona asked.

Her frown deepened. "No."

"Then you're single." Ava herded her to stand behind Emma who was pretending to wind up her throwing arm.

"Ready back there?" Emma asked.

"Ready," all the ladies, except Leslie, responded.

Emma flung the bouquet high into the air and behind her.

Arms rose into the air.

Leslie couldn't help it, she had to raise hers as well. With no clear intention of catching the bouquet, she watched as the bundle of flowers spun through the air as if in slow motion. When it hit its zenith, the bouquet tumbled downward, aiming toward someone else's arms, not hers. Jane, the tallest, smacked it to her left. Fiona batted at it like a volleyball and Ava leaped into the air, slam-dunking it into Leslie's outreached hands.

Leslie gasped as the flowers bounced off her fingers and landed against her chest. She couldn't believe she'd caught them. Nor could she believe the other ladies had gotten together to make certain she was the one who ended up with the pretty white roses.

A round of applause roared through the saloon.

Emma turned and smiled. "I can't think of a more perfect person to catch my bouquet," she said. "If it weren't for you and BODS, I might never have met Coop."

"And I wouldn't have met Gage," Fiona said.

"And I wouldn't have met Sean," Ava said.

"And I wouldn't have fallen in love with Moose," Jane said. "Leslie is responsible for the happiness of so many of us here tonight."

"That's right," Emma said, hurrying over to hug her. "You deserve to be as happy."

Leslie's eyes filled. "Thank you. All of you," she said. "It makes me very happy to see my clients and friends find love."

"And now, it's your turn to find love," Ava said. Her gaze shot to Tag, sitting on the sidelines with the other men. "And I think you have."

Fiona, Jane and Emma all turned to stare in the direction Ava was looking.

"So, will there be wedding bells between you and Tag?" Emma asked.

Leslie's face heated, fiery hot. "Oh, no. We're just friends," she said, out of habit, when her entire being wanted to be more than friends with her best friend.

"Ha. You've stepped over that line, sweetheart," Ava said.

Fiona nodded. "She's right, honey. You are so far past friend, if dancing without music is any indication."

"It is," Ava said.

Leslie shook her head. "We're very good friends."

Jane gave her a sly glance. "Friends with benefits?"

Her cheeks burning now, Leslie shook her head. "No, our relationship is nothing like that."

Emma snorted. "That's a shame. Maybe you should shake it up a bit. He looks willing."

"Yes, he does," Fiona said, her gaze on Tag.

"Stop," Leslie sputtered. "He's going to know

you're talking about him." She turned her back to him, her face on fire.

"We hope so. Then maybe he'll get cracking and make a move on you."

"If he hasn't already." Ave's eyes narrowed. "Has he?"

Leslie shook her head. "No, of course not. He's my friend."

"What part of friends with benefits do you not understand?" Emma asked.

"I tell you, we're not like that." Leslie drew in a deep breath. "Look, just let me get to my happy place on my own. I don't need your help to find a man, and Tag is not an appropriate option."

"The hell he isn't," Emma said. "He's kind, good-looking and loaded. What more could you ask for?"

Leslie turned enough to study Tag out of the corner of her eye. He was watching her, his brows meeting above his nose.

Tag was perfect. Like Emma said, he was kind, oh so handsome, and always had her back. Up until this past week, he'd been the one she'd shared all her ups and downs with. Now that she was considering him as someone other than just a friend, the dynamic of their relationship had changed. And she wasn't sure she was happy about that. She valued order in her existence, and everything about being with Tag was messy.

Emma hugged her. "Don't think yourself out of

anything, Leslie. You deserve a little happiness of your own." She glanced up at Coop, who stood beside Marjorie, waving at her. "Guess I'd better get going. My husband is getting restless." She grinned. "Coop's my husband. That sounds so strange, and yet, makes me happy." She hurried toward her groom, and they got ready to make their escape.

The guests lined up outside the saloon with bags of bird seed.

When Emma and Coop came out, a loud cheer went up and bird seed flew at the happy couple as they ran for Coop's pickup.

Some of the men had trashed it good with shaving cream, tin cans and streamers. On the back windshield were the words, *JUST HITCHED.*

Leslie couldn't be happier for Emma and Coop. And she was thrilled that BODS had brought them together.

Then why hadn't BODS worked for her? She and Tag had entered their data at the same time. They would have known immediately that they were a match.

BODS hadn't chosen them for each other.

"Ready to go home?" Tag said into her ear.

Leslie jumped and pressed a hand to her chest. Her pulse pounded so hard, she was certain he could hear it.

"I'm sorry if I startled you," Tag said. "You were so

deep in thought, I didn't think you'd hear me if I whispered."

"No, it's okay," she said. "And yes, I'm ready to go home."

He guided her through the throng of people standing around laughing and smiling at Emma and Coop as they drove out of the parking lot.

When they reached the truck, he opened the door for her and helped her up into the seat, tucking the hem of her gown around her to keep it from getting caught in the door. Once she was settled and buckled in, he rounded the pickup, giving Leslie a few precious moments to pull herself together.

Tag slid behind the wheel, started the engine and eased through the crowded parking lot to the highway.

Leslie stared at the bouquet of flowers in her lap for the duration of the drive back to Austin. She didn't know what to say or do. She wondered if Tag would kiss her when he dropped her off. If he did, how should she react? Shy and cautious? Sexy and encouraging? Or just plain panicked?

She was so wound up by the possibilities, she was on edge and ready to jump out of the truck when it pulled to a stop in front of her house. Her first instinct was to get out before Tag could come around to let her out. Her second instinct was to wait and let Tag help her down. At least then, he'd touch her, and possibly, let her slide down his body as he'd done before.

Heat coiled at her center.

When he opened her door, she waited for him to grip her around her waist and help her from her seat to the ground.

Instead, he offered her a hand.

What the hell?

She wanted the full body contact, not this impersonal and formal assist. Leslie considered faking a fall so that he had to catch her and hold her close. She chickened out at the last minute, afraid he'd miss, and she'd fall flat on her face on the pavement.

Gathering the hem of her dress in one hand, she took the outstretched hand and let him help her to the ground. So much for getting to press her body up against his. She'd thought they'd had something special going on the dance floor at the Ugly Stick Saloon. What had happened to cool his heels since then? Or had he come to his senses and realized he wasn't all that into her?

For a moment Leslie closed her eyes, desperate for answers, knowing she wouldn't get any from him. She wouldn't ask those questions, because she was too afraid she wouldn't like the response.

Still carrying the bouquet, she trudged up the front porch and stood in front of her door, fumbling with the key.

A big, warm hand settled on her arm and another reached for the keys. "Let me," he said.

She stepped to the side, allowing him access to the lock.

While he unlocked the door, she inhaled his scent. He smelled like expensive aftershave. His clean-shaven face of that morning now sported a heavy five o'clock shadow. Leslie wanted to know what the little bit of beard would feel like rubbing across her skin.

Tag pushed open the door and handed her the key, his fingers touching hers, causing a spark of electricity to fire through her system, rendering her speechless. This was it...the moment when he would kiss her, and she'd kiss him back.

He cupped her cheeks between his palms and bent his head.

Leslie tipped her chin upward and closed her eyes, ready to receive his sweet kiss.

He brushed her forehead with his lips.

Leslie frowned, opened her eyes and stared into his. "That's it?"

His brow wrinkled. "Is what it?"

She shook her head, clasped his face in her hands and pulled him down for a full-contact, no-holds-barred kiss. When he opened his lips, her tongue swept past his teeth, colliding with his in a sensuous dance of desire and discovery.

Her fingers laced into the thickness of his hair, drawing him closer still. She pressed her breasts to his chest. As much as she loved the way his suit felt against her skin, she wished they were naked.

His hand slid down her back and cupped her ass, pressing her tightly against his growing arousal. He wasn't so immune to her after all.

He lifted her, carried her across the threshold and kicked the door closed behind them. Slowly, he lowered her feet until they touched the ground, her dress riding up enough she could wrap her calf around his.

Oh, she wanted him. After four years of celibacy, she was hot and ready for more than a kiss. Leslie broke away, took his hand and started for her bedroom.

Tag took two steps and stopped, bringing her to an abrupt halt. "I can't," he said.

"What do you mean, you can't?" she asked, her frustration making her voice tight.

He shook his head. "I can't do this."

She frowned. "Can't because you have a medical condition, or won't because you changed your mind?"

"I can't because I respect you too much. This isn't what I wanted to happen tonight."

Leslie shoved a hand through her hair and stood alone on that floor, her heart crumbling into a thousand little pieces. "What you mean is, you don't want to."

"Not like this." He reached for her hands.

Leslie hid them behind her back and sighed heavily. "Just go."

"Leslie—"

"Please," she begged, her eyes filling with tears. "I'm tired to the bone, and I just want to sleep."

He started toward her and stopped, his hands falling to his sides. "I care about you, Leslie. More than you'll ever know. And for that reason, I'll do as you ask and go." Tag performed an abrupt about-face and left her house, closing the door softly behind him.

He left just in time for the tears to spill from Leslie's eyes and drench her cheeks.

They'd been so close to making love. Or at least, Leslie felt like they had. Then he'd changed his mind. Like a light switched off. That quickly, and that completely, leaving her in the dark for a reason why.

Had he remembered she was his best friend's wife? Had he had an attack of guilt, being in Randy's home, with Randy's wife? Or had he come to his senses and realized he didn't want to make love to her because she was a friend, not a potential lover?

Oh, but that kiss had been anything but a friend's kiss. It had been more passionate than anything Leslie had ever experienced, including the kisses she'd shared with Randy throughout their marriage. Those had been full of love and respect, not searing passion that ignited her soul.

Leslie let the tears fall as she stripped out of her

shoes, the red gown and her bra and panties. She ducked into the shower for a quick rinse and to wash the makeup from her face and the hairspray out of her hair. When she was finished, she stepped out of the shower, patted her skin dry and dressed in her unicorn pajamas. A quick trip to the kitchen to get a glass of water, and she was ready for bed.

Slipping between the sheets, she closed her eyes and imagined where the night would have gone had Tag not gone cold.

She lay for a long time, going over everything she'd said and done up to the point he'd suddenly backed away. They'd practically made love on the dance floor, fully clothed. What had stopped him when they were finally alone?

Leslie turned onto her side and punched her pillow. This was the reason she hadn't wanted to date again. Not only did she feel guilty for having a relationship with another guy, she wasn't even sure how to talk with men she'd never met before their first date. And thinking about her friend as a potential lover...

Why did dating have to be so hard?

She wasn't ready. That's all there was to it. And yet, she had a date scheduled for the next day. Thankfully, they'd be hiking. She wouldn't have to sit across a dinner table making small talk.

She leaned over to grab her laptop and opened it. A few quick clicks and she was online in the

BODS system. No new messages from Herman or Joe.

Other than watching her friends get married, it had been a disappointing day on the Leslie Lamb dating front.

She started to log off the BODS system when a message popped up from Joe Fox.

Her heart leaped and raced as she opened the email.

TAG HAD GONE STRAIGHT to his condo in downtown Austin and stripped naked, leaving a trail of tuxedo parts on the floor. A cool shower did little to douse the flames of desire eating a hole in his soul. He could have spent the night with Leslie. She'd made it clear that was what she wanted. But his conscience had cut the night short. After she'd ducked out the night before, he was afraid that if they made love, she'd have a tidal wave of regret the next morning. He didn't want their first time together to be remembered as a mistake. He wanted her to give herself to him without regret.

With so much pent-up emotion boiling below the surface, Tag couldn't sleep. He opened his laptop, brought up the BODS system and composed a message to Leslie that expressed his feelings without giving himself away.

Dear Leslie,

Fate has a way of putting obstacles in our path for a reason. Sometimes that reason isn't always obvious. Sometimes, the reason is to help us change into a better version of ourselves.

When I lost my love to another, I went through the stages of grief, including denial, anger, bargaining, depression and, finally, acceptance. Once I accepted that I'd lost her, I was able to let go. Not of her, but of me, the person I was. I reasoned that if I had not been the person I was, I might not have lost her. If I wanted to be a man worthy of another woman, I had to become a better version of me. So, I let go of the old me and set out to improve and become a better person. I like myself more and hope that, if I'm ever given another chance to love again, she will love the me I've become.

I can't completely regret my past because I wouldn't be the man I am without having gone through the struggle and transformation.

I guess what I'm saying is that your past is what makes you you. You don't have to forget it, in fact, remember it and learn. I learned not to give up on happiness, but to reach for it whenever I could. Sometimes it might mean taking it slowly, easing into it, when you want to grab and hold on. Trust your instincts and go for happiness in whatever form it presents itself. It's worth the struggle.

Joe

Before he could overthink his words, he sent the message.

For several long minutes, he tapped his fingers on

the edge of the laptop, wondering if Leslie had already gone to sleep. If not, would she log onto BODSand see his message? Part of him wanted her to, the other part of him didn't. He didn't usually wax poetic, but the situation called for it. As he'd written the words, he'd realized how much he'd changed from the man who'd lost Leslie to his best friend. For the better.

He hoped Leslie would see that and see him as someone other than a friend with benefits. His efforts weren't just to get her into bed. He wanted her for life.

He'd just about given up on seeing a response when a message popped up in his BODS inbox.

His heartbeat stuttered as he opened the email and read.

Dear Joe,

Thank you for being open and frank with me about your past and your loss. You're right that our pasts define us as individuals. When I lost my husband, I thought my world had ended. I was wrong. My husband's life ended, but mine kept going. Four years later, I'm still going and ready to let go of the past. Not of my memories of my husband and our lives together, because that time was special and made me realize how good life could be. My expectations are high because of him, and I won't settle for less. Though I could be happy with different.

I do have to let go of the past me and start living my life without my husband. I will always love him, because he will always be a part of me. But I have room in my heart to love again. I know this now. As my friends have all told me, I just have to be open to the possibility.

I enjoy our conversations. They make me think on a deeper level than I've allowed myself to go. Thank you for being you.

Leslie

Tag read the message again. And again. What did she mean that she had room in her heart to love again? Was she ready? Did she have someone in mind? Was it him as Tag Bronson, or her pen pal, Joe Fox? Or Bachelor Number One, Otis?

He didn't know where he stood with Leslie. He thought he'd had an idea when she'd invited him into her house and her bed. But her words to Joe left him wondering if she was in love with someone, or was still looking, keeping her options open.

Could she be falling in love with Joe Fox? And only wanted sex with Tag?

Tag's jaw hardened, a stab of jealousy ripping through him. Well, hell. He was jealous of himself. And afraid. Afraid she'd be disappointed it was him, when he finally unveiled his charade.

CHAPTER 11

LESLIE WAS surprised at how well she slept after she'd read and responded to Joe Fox's message. Something about his words resonated within her, calming her spirit and making her take a second look at her past and her current situation. It had been four years since she'd lost Randy. He'd told her to go on living, but she hadn't. Not really. Her love for him would never die, but she wanted to love again.

And she was entirely too wound up about dating through BODS and seeing Tag on a regular basis.

She needed to calm the hell down and let life happen.

With that in mind, she slept soundly, no dreams, no tumultuous thoughts, just much-needed rest.

When she woke the next morning, she dressed for a hike, had a cup of coffee and told herself she would have fun that day, no matter what. In her message to

Joe Fox, she'd said she'd be open to the possibilities. She might as well start today.

Before she set off on the two-hour drive to Enchanted Rock, she filled a water bottle full of ice and water, then texted Tag, letting him know she was leaving.

He texted back that he'd be there as soon as he and his date could get there. If she felt uncomfortable with her date, Tag said don't get into his car and stay around other people.

Leslie smiled. That was just like Tag to worry about her. He'd always had her back, even when she'd been married to Randy.

Leslie climbed into her SUV, set the directions on her GPS and took off on the day's adventure.

She hadn't been back to Enchanted Rock since she, Randy and Tag had gone all those years ago. Leslie smiled at the memory. At the very least, she'd get to hike the massive pink granite dome in central Texas. The sun was shining, the temperature would be warm, but not overbearingly hot. It promised to be a good day all around.

When she arrived at exactly ten o'clock in the parking lot, she parked her car, got out and stretched, looking around for a man who looked like the photo on BODS of Herman Lansing.

A man fitting his profile jogged toward her from the visitor's center, a smile on his face. He wore navy-blue running shorts, hiking boots and one of those red, moisture-wicking T-shirts runners loved. As well, he wore a small backpack.

He came to a stop in front of her and grinned. "You must be Leslie." He held out his hand.

She shook it and smiled up into his handsome face. "And you must be Herman."

"I am." He tipped his head toward the domed rock. "Have you been here before?"

Leslie shook her head. "Once. A long time ago. I'm looking forward to hiking it again."

"I love it. The hike isn't too hard, and the view is amazing."

"Yes, it is amazing," she agreed.

"I brought some snacks for lunch." He jerked his thumb over his shoulder, indicating the small backpack he had on his back. "I thought we'd take our time at the top. Did you bring a water bottle?"

"I did."

"Good. I forgot to tell you to do so. They have water refill stations along the way, if you run out." He grinned like a kid setting out on a field trip. "I'm ready if you are."

Leslie glanced around the parking lot, wishing Tag had arrived before they started out.

Herman was ready to go, and she had no real excuse for waiting.

"I'm ready."

"Then let's go." He turned and waited for her to

step up alongside him before he took off at a quick walk.

"Let me know if I'm walking too fast," he said. "It's a habit. I like to step out and cover the ground quickly."

So much for smelling the flowers along the way, Leslie thought. She skipped several times to keep pace with Herman. And they were still on the flat trail leading up to the base of the rock.

"So, you're a software developer?" Herman queried.

"I am."

"I'm a car salesman." He named one of the large dealerships in the Austin area. "I like it because it keeps me outside and up and moving throughout the day. In my off hours, I like to run, swim and ride bicycles. I'm training for an Ironman competition."

"I'm impressed. That takes some stamina."

He nodded. "I got hooked on fitness after high school. I'd gained a lot of weight and was very unhappy with my life. I saw my reflection in a window one day and hated what I'd become. So, I did something about it." He grinned. "I started running, and I haven't stopped."

"Apparently, it works for you," Leslie said, practically running to keep up with him. "You look great."

"Thanks. Are you into running?"

Leslie shrugged. "Not like you are. I work out three times a week, jogging on a track. I go two miles.

I learned to swim as a kid, but other than an occasional trip to the lake, I don't get to do much of that. As for biking…?" She shook her head. "I don't even own one right now."

Herman gave her a quick smile. "The nice thing about riding bicycles is that once you learn how, you never forget."

Leslie chuckled. "That's good, because I learned when I was in grade school, and I haven't been on a bike since then."

They arrived at the base of the domed rock where a variety of boulders in all sizes and shapes lay.

"This is where it gets a little harder," he said. "Let me know if you need help."

Leslie nodded. "Thanks."

They started up the trail.

At the pace Herman was moving, talk was out of the question for Leslie. She tried to keep up but found him waiting at several points along the trail upward.

She'd thought herself in fairly good shape. Ha! By the time she reached the top, she was sweating, not in a pretty, glowing way, but a full-on, gonna-die-soon way.

Herman gripped her arm, a frown denting his brow. "Are you okay?"

"I'm fine," she said between heaving breaths. "I just need to sit for a few minutes."

"Come over here. We can have a drink and munch on our lunch."

Lunch. Her stomach rumbled amid wanting to throw up. Leslie looked around at the dome-shaped summit, praying for a tree for a little much-needed shade.

What did she expect? Of course, there wasn't one. Enchanted Rock was a rock. Too tired to care, she dropped where she was and lay flat on her back, dragging air into her lungs.

Herman's eyebrows drew together as he studied her. "Are you sure you're okay?"

Leslie shaded her eyes and stared up at the handsome man, wanting to throat punch him. The bastard hadn't even broken a sweat and wasn't breathing hard in the least.

"I'm fine," she said, though her tone was a little harsh. She closed her eyes and said in a softer voice, "Really. I just need to rest for a moment. I'm not in nearly as good shape as you are."

"It's okay," he said, dropping down to sit beside her. "I don't always remember that when I'm with others. You should have said something. I would have slowed down." He slipped the pack off his shoulders and handed her the bottle of water she'd been foresighted enough to bring. "Here, drink. You look like you could use it."

In other words, she looked like hell. Great first impression. Leslie took the bottle, struggled to sit up and drank half of it down, nearly choking as she did.

"Hey, slow down," Herman said. He pulled a neatly wrapped granola bar out of his backpack. "You can munch on that for energy."

"I'd rather wait for lunch."

He grimaced. "This is lunch. I didn't think we'd need anything heavy while hiking."

At that moment, Leslie could have eaten a whole bucket of fried chicken by herself. She sighed and took the offering. Instead of opening it, she uncapped her water bottle and guzzled more of the refreshing, lukewarm water.

When she felt a little more like herself, she looked around at the other hikers walking across the smooth granite summit.

When she glanced back in the direction from which they'd come, she spotted Tag and a pretty brunette coming up over the rise. The brunette was bouncy and smiling, dressed in running shorts, sneakers, a sports bra and a loose tank top. Her hair was pulled back in a long ponytail, and she looked like she was having a great time. Tag was smiling at something she said.

Bitch. Leslie glared at her, an uncontrollable anger burning away at her normally kind and gentle spirit. How could that woman be smiling and bouncing after climbing up that horrible, treacherous trail?

Tag's gaze swept the top of the rise and found her.

His grin turned downward, and a frown settled heavily on his brow. He gripped his date's elbow and steered her toward Leslie and Herman. "Leslie?" he said. "Is that you?"

She wanted to snap back, *Of course, it's me. You knew I was coming.* Instead, she bit back her immediate response and said, "Tag?"

"What an incredible coincidence to see you way out here. It's a small world." He turned to his date. "Chrissy, this is a good friend of mine, Leslie Lamb. Leslie, Chrissy Trent."

Chrissy smiled broadly and held out her hand.

Leslie struggled to her feet, the muscle in the back of her right calf screaming as she put weight on it. She would have fallen but for Herman's hand shooting out to capture her arm. She gave him a tight smile. "Thanks. I got a little off balance." She forced a smile to her lips and took Chrissy's hand in hers. "Nice to meet you, Chrissy." She turned to her date. "This is Herman Lansing, my date."

"Nice to meet you, Chrissy." Herman held out his hand to Chrissy, taking in her appearance head to toe, and pausing at her running shoes. "Oh, you like Hokas?"

She nodded. "I usually run in these, but thought they'd be okay for a hike."

He nodded. "That's my brand of choice for marathons."

Her eyes widened along with her grin. "You run marathons?"

Herman nodded. "I do."

"I thought I was the only nutcase who did that. I'm really glad to meet another running enthusiast." She looked around the dome. "Is this your first time up here?"

Herman shook his head. "No, I come up often. I like to race up the trail and try to improve my time every visit."

Leslie moaned softly.

Herman laughed and cast Leslie an amused glance. "Not that I did this time. I kept my pace slow since I wasn't sure how much climbing you've done."

Leslie sighed. "Now, you know."

"This is my first time here. I think I'll look around," Chrissy said. She glanced at Tag. "You don't have to come, if you'd like to catch up with your friend."

"I'll go with you," Herman said.

Chrissy didn't wait for Tag's response. She walked off with Herman.

"Are you signed up for the half-marathon next weekend in Austin?" Herman was asking as they moved away.

Leslie dropped back down before she fell and rubbed at the calf muscle that had seized while she was standing. "This was a bad idea."

"I don't know. It's a beautiful day, and the view is amazing."

"I hiked up with Ironman Lansing," she whined. "I thought I was going to die of a heart attack by the time we got to the top." She rolled her eyes. "And he slowed down for me."

Tag chuckled and sat in front of her. "Here, let me." He brushed her hands aside and massaged her calf, digging his fingers into the muscles, gently at first, and then harder as he worked out the stiffness. "You should have gone at your own pace."

"I thought I was, but he had to stop so many times, I felt bad." She watched as his hand worked at the muscle, wishing he would apply the same massage technique to her entire body.

In bed. Naked.

Her cheeks heated at the thought. Afraid he'd see her lusty thoughts in her eyes, she shifted her gaze to Chrissy and Herman talking nonstop with each other as they walked across the broad dome of Enchanted Rock.

"What's with Chrissy? Is she also into marathons and triathlons?" Leslie asked.

Tag's mouth twisted. "As a matter of fact, she is."

"How could BODS get this so wrong? I am not into running for miles and miles. Two miles is my limit. Even then, I'm huffing and puffing." She shook her head. "I have to get in better shape." She frowned at him. "And why aren't you breathing hard?"

"I work outside a lot on my ranch. I guess it's enough to keep me in shape." He looked away. "And I have a home gym when the weather is bad."

"That's it. I'm joining a gym." Leslie lay back on the granite. "Right after I eat my way through an entire pizza by myself and get a helicopter to bring me down off this rock."

"Are you hungry?" Tag asked.

She looked up. "Starving." Leslie held up the granola bar Herman had handed her. "This was his idea of lunch."

Tag chuckled. "I'm afraid I wasn't thinking healthy. I brought a bag full of fried chicken, and my date is vegan. Want some?"

"God, yes," she said, sitting up with renewed enthusiasm.

He opened the bag and let her choose her poison.

Leslie selected a breast and bit into the greasy, salty mess, moaning softly. "I was so hungry. The granola bar wasn't going to do it for me," she said around the bite in her mouth.

"Glad I could be of assistance." He selected a drumstick and dug in. "I tried to be on time, but Chrissy couldn't locate her running shoes. She finally found them beneath a gym bag she'd left in the back of her car last night."

"Better late than never," Leslie said. "Especially since you came bearing gifts." She grinned over her huge piece of chicken. "Thank you."

For the next few minutes, Leslie filled her belly, thankful for the food to keep her from having to come up with conversation.

When she'd had enough, she sighed and wiped her hands on a sanitary wipe Tag'd had the foresight to bring along with the chicken. "You thought of everything," she said.

"Not everything," he said with a grimace. "I didn't think to ask Chrissy if she liked fried chicken. I assumed everyone did."

Leslie tipped her head toward Chrissy and Herman. "I think I need to be more specific when I say I like the outdoors. I like it in a stroll-through-the-park way, or a let's go for a leisurely trail ride on well-trained horses kind of way. I don't feel like I have to beat my record every time I climb to the top of a hill."

"It's admirable to stretch your limits," Tag said.

"I do that every day with my brain. I don't feel like I have to do it with my body." She rubbed her calf and flexed her toes. "And we still have to get down off this rock."

Tag nodded toward Chrissy and Herman heading their way. "Think we've matched another pair?"

Leslie smiled. "Yes. I need to review the code in BODS. That's the second time it's missed for both of us."

"Do you get the feeling it's testing us?" Tag said.

Leslie looked up at him, her eyes narrowing. "For what?"

"To see if we're really ready. Maybe it's giving us matches that are off just a little, working our way through a few to get to the right one."

"It's a computer program, not artificial intelligence." She shook her head. "If that were the case, your next match would be your perfect match."

"And Bachelor Number Four would be yours." He met her gaze. "Maybe we should have skipped to the last."

Leslie didn't get a chance to respond to his statement before Chrissy and Herman joined them. The two runners shared stories about some of the events they'd participated in as they ate granola bars and drank water. Though they tried to include Leslie and Tag in the conversation, if it didn't have to do with running, biking or swimming, they weren't that interested.

At one point, Tag asked Chrissy if she'd ever been to a Comic Con. Her brow had wrinkled as she shook her head. "Never. That kind of thing doesn't interest me."

"How about you, Herman?" Leslie asked.

"I wouldn't mind going just to see what it's like, but I've been to so many automobile conventions, it just gets old. I prefer to be outside, rather than surrounded inside a convention hall."

Leslie nodded, finally finding something they could agree on.

When the granola bars were consumed and the wrapping safely stowed in Herman's backpack, Herman glanced down at Leslie. "Ready to head back down?"

She nodded. "But don't wait on me. I'll be taking my time." She held out her hand. "It's been a pleasure. Thank you for suggesting Enchanted Rock. It gave me a reason to visit."

"I don't want to leave you alone," Herman said.

"I can go down with her," Tag said. He glanced at Chrissy. "If you don't mind. Or you can go down with Herman, if we're too slow."

Chrissy looked from Tag to Leslie. "Are you sure? I'll wait for you at the bottom."

Herman stepped up beside her. "You're from Austin, aren't you?"

The brunette nodded. "I am."

Herman faced Tag. "I can get her home, if you two are going to be a while."

Tag chuckled. "You two seem to be hitting it off better with each other than with us." He held up a hand when Chrissy and Herman shook their heads. "It's not going to hurt my feelings."

"Nor mine," Leslie said. "I'm just glad you two have so much in common. And since I drove, I'll be driving myself home anyway.

"If Chrissy doesn't mind, I don't mind," Tag said.

"Great." Chrissy grinned. She held out her hand to Tag. "Thank you for suggesting this outing. I had a great time."

"You're welcome." Tag gave her a crooked grin. "It was nice to meet you both."

Chrissy and Herman hurried away, leaving Tag and Leslie to make their way slowly down the dome to the trail leading back to the parking lot. Tag helped Leslie over the big boulders by lending a hand when she needed one or gripping her around the waist and lowering her to the trail beside him.

Every time he touched her, she was reminded of the night before and how Tag had backed away when she'd clearly indicated she wanted to make love with him. Her libido had been charged and ready. Tag must have had second thoughts. He was back to being the friend he'd always been. She bet if she tried to kiss him again, he'd be appalled.

When they reached their vehicles, there was no sign of Herman and Chrissy.

Leslie faced Tag, her heart hurting for what couldn't be. She was willing, but they both had to be on board to make it happen. Tag clearly wasn't on the same path. She held out her hand. "Well, thank you for being here. I'm sure I would have been fine with Herman. He seemed very nice. Not for me, but nice."

Tag gripped her hand. "I'm glad we were able to connect him and Chrissy. They seemed made for each other," Tag said. He stared at his hand wrapped around hers. Then he pulled her into a hug. "As always, it's good to be with you." He held her for a short moment, and then set her at arms' length, dropping his hands to his side. "I'll follow you back to Austin."

"That's not necessary," she said.

"I have to get there anyway. I might as well." He waved a hand toward her SUV.

Leslie didn't like the way their day was ending. She didn't want to say goodbye. Not yet. She wanted to be with Tag so much it hurt. How could she remain friends with the man when she wanted to be more than friends? "Do you have plans for dinner?" she blurted.

He shook his head. "No."

"I make a mean lasagna," she said. "I can never finish the whole thing by myself. Could you help a girl out and come to dinner?"

"You know, I haven't had your lasagna in forever." He nodded. "I'd like that."

Her heart swelled. "Okay. I have most of the ingredients at the house. I only have to stop for one or two items."

"I'll help you. I can pick the wine."

She smiled. Really happy for the first time that day.

On the drive to Austin, Tag called her on her cellphone. Using the handsfree option on their vehicles, they talked about BODS, the wedding and their first two dates all the way back. He had her laughing and joking like old times.

A quick stop at the grocery store was accomplished by a dash through the aisles for ingredients and wine. Leslie couldn't remember having more fun shopping for groceries than she had that day with Tag.

By the time they reached her house, she had built up her hopes that he would stay for dinner, and then for breakfast the next morning. It was a lot to hope for, given how he'd left the night before, but Leslie couldn't help it. She wanted Tag to stay so badly, she would will it to happen.

What better way to please a man, than through his stomach first? And then…

CHAPTER 12

TAG CARRIED the bag of groceries and wine into the house and set them on the counter. He hadn't planned on coming to dinner at Leslie's house. He'd wanted to give her more time to think about what she wanted in a man, and then come to the obvious conclusion that man was him. He still wasn't sure she was ready for the next step, but he told himself they didn't have to go there tonight.

She needed at least one more date to know for sure. He'd bring it up after dinner. In the meantime, he would enjoy being with her. And by being with her, he'd show her that he could be everything she wanted and needed.

When she went out with Bachelor Number Three, she'd know he wasn't right for her.

Together, they cooked the meat, mixed in the tomato sauce and all the spices. Tag got a pot of lasagna noodles boiling and made every opportunity he could to reach around Leslie he could, brushing his arms against hers and touching her hands to trade spoons and spatulas. By the time the lasagna was baking in the oven, he was so aroused he had to sit at the table to hide it.

"When are you going to go out with your next date?" he asked.

The smile she'd worn since they'd left the grocery store slipped. "I hadn't even thought about it."

"You shouldn't let today make you hesitate," he said.

"I don't know. I'm beginning to think BODS isn't working."

"Consider it one more beta test. If your next date as equally disastrous, you'll know you need to tweak the code."

Her lips twisted into a grimace. "I really don't know if I'm up to another date so soon."

"Think of it as an adhesive bandage."

Her brow furrowed. "You mean, like, I know it's going to hurt so I should just rip it off?" Leslie laughed. "You're not making a good case for me to go on my next date. And what about you? When are you going to go out with your third match?" She cocked an eyebrow in challenge.

He held up his phone. "I'll do it right now," he said. "And you?"

She sighed. "Fine, but only because I want to beta

test BODS." She checked the oven timer, then hurried out of the kitchen. She was back a minute later with her laptop. In seconds, she had BODS up. "I think you had a point about skipping to the end. I think since you're at your last match, I'm going to skip to mine."

Tag frowned. She wasn't heading the direction he'd expected. "Are you sure you want to skip past Milton? He might be the one."

She shook her head. "No, I think I've had enough. One more is all I'm going for."

"I thought number four didn't want to meet right away."

"He didn't, but it's about time we met." She clicked away on her keyboard.

Tag turned away so that she couldn't see what he was doing on his cellphone. He brought up the BODS application in time to see her message come across. He opened it and quickly read it.

Joe,

I think it's time we met.

Leslie

IT WASN'T part of his plan, but he could make this work. He responded.

Leslie,

I agree. How does Friday work for you?

Joe

. . .

LESLIE LOOKED UP AND FROWNED. "He wants to meet on Friday."

Tag shrugged. "Sounds good. I'm sure I can make it work with my date."

"That's not good," Leslie said. "I want to get this over with."

"What are you thinking?" Tag asked, feeling guilty that he was playing her. He hoped she wouldn't be mad when she finally learned he was Joe.

Leslie shook her head. "The sooner the better." She bent to her keyboard, her fingers clicking furiously.

Joe,

Friday doesn't work for me. Could you make it Monday night?

Leslie

TAG FOUGHT A GRIN. "What did you tell him?"

"I want Monday night. I hope he goes for it."

LESLIE,

Wednesday would be better. If that's good for you, I'll meet you at Rosa's Patio at seven o'clock.

Joe

. . .

Leslie frowned.

"Is he going for it?" Tag asked, knowing full well he was pushing her to Wednesday.

"No. He wants Wednesday and to meet at Rosa's Patio at seven o'clock."

"I like that place. Their margaritas are the best," Tag said. "I'll see if my date can do the same."

"I guess it'll be okay." Leslie's frown deepened. "Problem is, I don't know what he looks like." She tapped away on her keyboard again.

Wednesday is good. *How will I know you? I don't have a clear photo to go by.*
Leslie

"With a name like Joe Fox, he'll probably have a red rose at the table," Tag said as he tapped his screen with his response. "My date is on for Wednesday."

Leslie,
I'll be the man with a yellow rose lying on the table.
Joe

. . .

LESLIE GLANCED UP, her brow furrowed. "He's going to have a yellow rose. What does that mean?"

"Why does the color have to mean anything?" Tag asked. He'd picked the color to be something different than the red he'd teased about. He spoke to his phone. "Siri, what are the meanings for the colors of roses?"

His cellphone came back with a webpage displaying the colors of roses and their meanings. He leaned close to Leslie with the display and enlarged the image. "Yellow roses mean welcome back."

Her frown deepened.

Tag scrolled down a little farther, breathed a sigh and pointed. "And it also means new beginnings."

Her frown eased. "New beginnings. Okay, I guess that's okay. Not that I plan on starting anything with Joe. I'm over this matchmaking BODS came up with. I have to work on the software. I hate to think it might be this far off on other matches, besides ours."

"I'm sure it's okay. Look at our friends," Tag said. "They're ecstatic."

Leslie smiled. "They are, aren't they?"

"And look at the people we matched up on our first two dates. They were perfect for each other."

"I'll have to see if they would have been matched together eventually, anyway," she said. "I like to think I kept an open mind to the possibilities, but neither one was a fit for me. How about you?"

Tag held up his hand. "Me, either. I had more fun

being with you than with them." He took her hand in his. "Have you ever wondered what would have happened if you hadn't married Randy?"

Her frown was back. "What do you mean?"

He stared down at her fingers, rubbing his thumb over her knuckles. "Have you ever thought about what we could have meant to each other?" He looked up into her eyes, pinning her with his gaze.

She sucked in a swift breath and bit down on her bottom lip. "No."

A red-hot poker stabbed him in the heart. It wasn't quite the answer he'd hoped for. "Oh, okay." He started to let go of her hand.

She curled her fingers around his. "I hadn't thought of you and me before I married Randy. You never seemed interested. But you've always been there for me, for us. Our friend."

"Was that all you ever thought of me as..." he lifted her hand to his lips and pressed his lips to her fingertips, "as a friend?"

"I think a best friend is a really good place to start," she whispered, her eyes filling with tears.

"Did you know I was in love with you back when the three of us met all those years ago?"

She shook her head, the tears spilling from her eyes. "No. I never knew."

"I was."

Her eyes widened. "Was?"

"The me of so long ago fell in love with the you of

back then. We've both changed. And I realized Randy was the right choice for you, at that time." He smiled into her eyes. "And now, I have you as my best friend. I wouldn't change that for anything.

She smiled through her tears. "I'm glad I have you as my best friend, too."

He brushed a tear away from her cheek. "Then why are you crying?"

"I don't know." She wiped her face with both hands. "Maybe they're happy tears. A girl can cry happy tears, can't she?"

"As long as they're happy." He pulled her into his arms and held her close. "One more date. This one might be the one for you."

"You, too." Her arms tightened around his neck. "And then what about us? How will our significant others feel about you and me being friends?"

"We'll cross that bridge when we get to it," he said. He gripped her arms and set her away. "For now, we're still friends, and I'm here for you."

Leslie nodded. "Thank you."

He chuckled. "For what?"

"For all you do for me."

"I'd do it no matter what. You're my friend, and I love you."

Her eyes flared briefly.

He hadn't meant to tell her he loved her yet. Hopefully, couching it with being his friend made it less scary for her. He didn't know her true feelings for him. If she didn't love him as more than a friend, he didn't want to make things awkward between them by confessing his undying love for her.

He was walking a fine line. He didn't want to lose her. If all she wanted was to be his friend, he'd be disappointed, but that wouldn't change his desire to be close to her.

After finishing his meal, he pushed back from the table and stood. "I'd better get going. We both have to work tomorrow. I'll see you Wednesday," he said.

"You won't be into my office before then?" she asked.

"I have some corporate meetings Monday and Tuesday. Though I have people to run my corporation, they like it when I show up. It lets them know I care."

Leslie took his hand and walked with him to the door. "Are you sure you don't want to stay for coffee or a nightcap?"

He wanted to stay but knew he had to let her think about her last date and whether she would match with him, if she even wanted to.

When he reached the door, she pulled him to a stop.

"I wish you didn't have to leave," she whispered.

He gripped both of her hands in his. "I'm always a phone call away."

"Sometimes, that isn't near enough," she said.

"Are you feeling Randy's loss?"

She shrugged. "I'll always miss him, but no, that's not it. I guess I'm just feeling a little lonely."

He pulled her in for another hug, loving the feel of her body against his. He was tempted to stay. So very tempted.

After holding her for a long time, he kissed her forehead and smiled down at her. "I'll see you Wednesday." He opened the door and left, closing the door between them.

For another long moment, he stood staring at her door, wondering if he was an idiot. He could have stayed. They might have made love.

And he might have blown their entire relationship because he was moving too fast.

Tag sucked in a deep breath, performed an about face and left.

Wednesday was D-Day. He'd see her then. Hopefully, his plan would work, she'd realize she loved him as more than a friend and she wouldn't be curious about any other date BODS might match her with.

Or all his plans could blow up in his face, she could be beyond angry with him for leading her on with his Joe Fox persona and their friendship could be a thing of the past.

Tag's gut knotted. He'd know soon enough.

CHAPTER 13

"Woman, do you ever stop pacing?" Ava walked into Leslie's office, carrying the mail she'd already gone through.

Leslie stopped in front of the floor-to-ceiling windows overlooking downtown Austin and faced her assistant and friend. "I can't help it."

"Tonight's the night, isn't it?" Ava smiled and laid the papers on Leslie's desk. "Your final date. Are you excited?"

Leslie sucked in a deep breath and let it out in a rush. "No. I don't want to go. I know in my heart who I want to be with, and I don't know how to tell him." Tears welled in her eyes.

"And that who is…?"

"You know."

She smiled. "Tag?"

Leslie nodded.

Ava squealed and hugged herself. "I knew it."

Leslie's brow pinched. "You knew?"

"Of course, I knew," Leslie said. "It was obvious to everyone but you."

"Everyone?" Leslie cover her mouth with her hands. "Even Tag?"

Ava frowned. "I'm not sure about Tag, but the rest of us could see it."

"I love him. I don't want to be with anyone else." She flung her hands in the air. "What am I going to do?"

Ava hurried over to Leslie and gathered her in her arms. "It's okay. You don't have to go out with Joe. You can cancel the date."

"It's too late," Leslie wailed. "I don't have his phone number."

"Then email him. Tell him you've had a death in the family and can't make it."

"What if he doesn't get the email in time?" She shook her head. "He'd be at that restaurant, expecting me to show up. What a horrible thing it is to be stood up." She shook her head. "I can't do that."

"At least, try to email him." Ava led her to her desk and guided her into her seat. She leaned over her shoulder and brought up the BODS application. "Go on, give it a shot. He might be online." Ava snatched a tissue from the box on Leslie's desk and pressed it into her hand.

Leslie wiped her eyes, blew her nose and tossed

the tissue into the trash bin. Then she squared her shoulders and logged into BODS. As soon as her profile came up, she saw that she had a message from Joe. "He's messaged me," she whispered.

"Maybe he's cancelling," Ava said. "Open it."

Leslie opened the message and read it out loud.

Dear Leslie,

I can't tell you how much I'm looking forward to meeting you at last. I didn't know how I'd feel about being matched with someone through BODS, and I appreciate your patience and your communications before we actually meet in person. I love that we seem to have more in common on a deeper level than I've had with most women. I'm hopeful for our future but don't feel pressured. No matter how this ends up, know that I am eternally grateful for the chance to get to know you better. You're an amazing woman, and you deserve a lifetime full of love and happiness whether it's with me or someone else.

Very truly yours,

Joe Fox

Leslie leaned back and groaned. "I can't do it. I can't cancel our date. Not after a letter like that."

"Yes, you can," Ava urged. "Just put your fingers on the keyboard and tell him you've changed your mind about everything."

Leslie shook her head. "I can't. That's not something I can do in an email. He's been so kind. I can't be that cold." She straightened. "I'll go, but I won't stay. I'll tell him I'm not interested, but that he shouldn't give up. Oh, hell." She pressed a hand to her lips. "Tag's supposed to be there with his date."

"So, bust them up," Ava said, planting her fists on her hips. "Tag's *your* man."

She shook her head. "He's not my man. He's my friend." Her gaze met Ava's. "What if that's all he wants from me? Friendship. What if he doesn't love me the way I love him?"

"Oh, sweetie. How could he not love you?" Ava smiled down at her. "It'll be all right. His date can't be a better match for him than you."

"But BODS chose her for him. I wasn't even in his lineup." Leslie at her monitor. "Why didn't I show up as his match?"

"Don't worry about it." Ava turned Leslie's chair around so that she couldn't look at her monitor. "You love him, don't you?"

She nodded. "More than I ever thought I could love again."

"Then you have to tell him."

"When?" Leslie asked. "He's got a date tonight."

"Have him over for dinner tomorrow night."

Leslie shook her head. "I had him over on Sunday night."

"Go to his condo, knock on his door and blurt it out," Ava suggested.

Leslie's brow wrinkled. "He might not be there. He goes out to his ranch more often than not."

"Go to his office, strip naked and make love with

him on his desk." Ava flung her hands in the air. "I don't know. Just do it."

Leslie's hands tightened into fists. "You're right. I won't know where he stands until I tell him how I feel." She looked up at Ava, her jaw tightening. "I'll do it."

"When?"

"I'll call him after his date tonight. He'll want to know why I left the restaurant without eating dinner. And I can ask him how his date went." She nodded. "Then I'll see if he's going to his condo or the ranch."

Ava grimaced. "And if he's going alone."

Leslie's eyes widened. "Oh, God, what if he's not alone? What if his date is his perfect match?"

Ava took her hands. "Don't borrow trouble. The other two dates haven't worked out. This one won't either. Think positive."

"What if she is his perfect match?" Leslie buried her face in her hands. "I couldn't come between them. Not if she makes him happy. I love him that much. I want him to be happy, with me or without me."

"Sweetie, you're borrowing trouble." She pulled Leslie's hands away from her face. "Pull yourself together and plan for your happily ever after outcome." She handed her another tissue. "Now, wipe your face and get ready to go home, shower, change and get to the restaurant on time."

Leslie wiped her face and pushed back from her desk. "You're right. I have to do this."

Ava left Leslie's office, returning to her own. A deep voice sounded from within that made Leslie's gut knot and her heart race.

"Ava, good to see you. Is Leslie in her office?"

"Tag, I didn't know you would be coming in today," Ava said loud enough for Leslie to overhear her clearly. "Yes, of course, Leslie's here. We were just about to close up shop and head home."

Leslie grabbed her compact out of her purse and gasped at her reflection. Her eyes were puffy, and she had a smear of mascara below one of them. She rubbed the mascara and dabbed powder on her face to mask the tracks of her tears.

"Come on back," Ava was saying. "She'll be happy to see you."

Leslie shoved her compact into her purse and sat up straight in her chair.

Ava led Tag to her office and stood by the door as he passed through it.

"Hey," Tag said.

Leslie stared at his beloved face, gulped and replied, "Hey."

Behind Tag, Ava was mouthing the words, *Tell him!*

Leslie gave a brief, hopefully imperceptible shake of her head. "Thank you, Ava. You don't have to wait for me. I'm sure you need to be heading out to pick up Mica from the daycare." She prayed Ava would take the hint and leave.

Ava pursed her lips and pointed her finger at Leslie.

Tag turned toward Ava.

Ava dropped her hand and smiled broadly at Tag. "I'll be going. You two don't do anything I wouldn't do." She winked at Tag and smiled at Leslie. "I'll see you tomorrow."

Leslie nodded and waited for Ava to leave them alone.

The door to the outer office opened and closed, leaving Leslie and Tag alone.

"I stopped by to let you know I won't be bringing my date to the restaurant tonight."

Leslie's heart dropped into her shoes. On one hand, she was glad he wasn't going to date his Bachelorette Number Three and fall in love with her. On the other hand, he wouldn't be at the restaurant to fake a double date. Not that she was going to stay. Leslie sighed. "That's too bad. Did she say why?"

Tag shook his head. "Not a word."

"I'm sorry." She wasn't really. Just sad he wouldn't be there.

"I'm sure you'll be all right. Give Joe a chance. And if things don't work out, you can call me and let me know." His lips twisted. "Either way, call me and let me know you got home all right."

She nodded. "I will," she said past the lump in her

throat. "Are you going to try to go out with your date another time?"

"I don't know," he said. "I'll give it a day or two and see how I feel. Your main concern is tonight. Focus on this date. If you're open to the possibilities, it might be your lucky night." He took her hand. "No matter what, I hope we will always be friends."

She nodded. "I hope so, too." And if he didn't leave soon, she'd burst into tears. Ava's entreaty to tell him that she loved him roiled in her gut. She didn't feel right telling Tag she loved him until her slate was clear and she'd broken it to Joe that she was in love with another man. As soon as she did that, she would call or go by Tag's place and open herself to the possibilities of loving Tag. She prayed he would be there, and that he wouldn't think she was ridiculous.

"Will you be staying the night in Austin?" Leslie asked.

"I have a meeting tonight. After that, I don't know. It depends on how my meeting goes." He raised her hand to his lips and pressed a kiss to her knuckles. "I hope everything turns out great tonight, and that whatever happens, you'll be happy."

"Thank you. I'll call you later," Leslie said.

"Can I walk you to your car?"

Leslie nodded. "I'd like that."

He waited for her to gather her purse and lock the office door. Together, they traveled down the elevator to the parking garage. He walked her to her SUV and waited as she opened the door.

"Remember to be open to the possibilities," he repeated and kissed her knuckles again.

"I'll try," she said and climbed into her Lexus, closed the door and started the engine.

Tag walked to his truck and waved at her as she passed by him.

Leslie kicked herself all the way to her house. She should have told him she loved him. Why had she balked? She knew next to nothing about Joe, and he wasn't the one she loved. Tag was the man she wanted to spend the rest of her life with, to grow old and gray with. Joe was sweet, and he said all the right things, but Tag was the one who'd been with her through thick and thin. He'd admitted that he'd loved her once. Surely, he could love her again.

Leslie dressed in a simple black dress and sexy heels. If Tag's meeting went well, and he stayed in Austin, she might stop by his place after she broke it to Joe that she wasn't going to stay for dinner or anything else. She hated that she'd be disappointing the man after he'd been so nice and said all those lovely things in his messages. But she had to do it. She loved Tag.

As she neared the restaurant, her belly clenched and churned. She wished Tag had been able to come tonight. She always felt better knowing he would be there.

She climbed out of her Lexus and closed the door, hitting the lock button on the handle. Five minutes, and she'd be back in her vehicle, driving toward Tag's penthouse apartment. Five minutes, and she'd be on her way to tell him that she loved him.

Squaring her shoulders, she entered Rosa's Patio and looked around. The restaurant was divided into many different sections, designed to give each customer a little privacy. She'd been here before with Tag after Randy had passed away. Tag had brought her here to cheer her up. She'd enjoyed the food and the ambiance. She thought it ironic that Joe had chosen a place she'd been to with Tag.

The hostess greeted her with a smile. "How many in your party?"

Leslie blinked. "Two. But I think my date might already be here."

"Name?" the hostess asked.

"Joe Fox," Leslie said.

She nodded. "He's waiting for you on the patio. Do you know where that is?"

Leslie nodded.

More guests entered behind Leslie.

"I can find it myself," she assured the hostess.

"Thank you," the young woman said. "Enjoy your evening."

Leslie weaved her way through the maze of tables and alcoves toward the back patio. She paused as she reached the door leading outside and stared through the big windows out into the open. She stood for a moment, studying the people seated out there. One table had a couple sitting together, hands entwined. Another table had four women drinking margaritas. Another table was blocked partially by a large potted plant with big palm fronds. On the table lay a single yellow rose.

Leslie's heart skipped several beats and her hands tightened into fists. That had to be the table where Joe Fox was sitting. Waiting for her. She wished this meeting was already over so she could tell Tag how much she loved him and wanted to be with him.

She drew in a steadying breath and held it. Then she stepped toward the door.

"Leslie," a familiar voice said behind her. "I'm glad I caught you."

Leslie turned to face Tag.

She let go of the breath she'd been holding in a rush. "Tag. I didn't think you were coming."

"I wanted to catch you before you met Joe Fox." He captured her hands in his. "There's something you should know."

Leslie stared up into his eyes, her heart swelling so large she thought it might burst from her chest. "And there's something I need to tell you."

He pressed his lips together in line and nodded. "Ladies, first."

Leslie stared up at him, her pulse hammering through her veins. "Tag, I can't go through with this date. I came to tell Joe Fox that I won't be able to go out with him."

"Why?" he asked.

"Because…" She licked her lips and threw herself into her confession with all her heart. "Because I already love someone else."

Tag stood completely still, his hands tightening around hers. "Are you sure?"

She nodded, her eyes filling, a crooked smile twisting her lips. "I'm absolutely sure."

"Do I know this person?" he asked softly.

She nodded. "Tag Bronson, it's you. I love you. I didn't realize just how much until I logged onto BODS and tried to find my perfect match." She shook her head. "I didn't realize I already had. I was so blind. But now I see. You're my perfect match." She frowned, tears leaking from her eyes. "Oh, Tag, say something. I know you said you would always be my friend, but I want more. I want you as my best friend, my lover and my life mate. Please, talk to me. Please love me."

His mouth claimed hers, cutting off her flow of words with a kiss that rocked her soul and took her breath away.

She wrapped her arms around his neck and pulled him as close as two people in a restaurant could be without being naked.

When he finally raised his head, he stared down into her eyes. "Is it my turn?" he asked.

She laughed, the sound catching in her throat. "That's right, you wanted to tell me something."

He cupped her cheeks in his palms. "I wanted you to know that I loved you way back when we first met."

The tears flowed harder. "And you don't love me now?"

He shook his head. "Not like I loved you then." He brushed the moisture from her cheek. "I love you even more. I'm a different man from the Tag who hung out with you and Randy. I know what's important now. I don't want to go another day without you in my life."

She wrapped her arms around him and held him close. "I never thought I could love another as much as I loved Randy."

"And now?" Tag asked.

"And now, I know I can love someone else as much, but in a different way."

Tag brushed a strand of her hair back behind her ear. "I will never ask you to stop loving Randy. He was my friend, and I loved him, too."

"I could never stop loving him. But I want to move on with my life. I know now that I have enough room in my heart to love again." She grasped his face in both of her hands. "And I love you."

Tag smiled down at her. "I was so afraid you would only ever see me as your friend."

She laughed. "I was afraid of the same."

"I think Randy would have been happy for us," Tag said. "He only ever wanted you to be happy."

She nodded. "He told me not to grieve too long, to find someone else to love. I think he would have approved of my choice."

"What about Joe?"

She smiled up at him. "Joe who?" Then she blinked. "Oh, dear." She looked past Tag to the yellow rose draped across the table on the patio. "I'm supposed to be with Joe tonight. I need to tell him I can't."

"I don't think that's necessary," Tag said.

Leslie shook her head. "I can't let him think I stood him up." She stepped around Tag and started through the door. "I'll be right back. It will only take me a minute."

Tag followed her. "Really, Leslie. It's not necessary."

By then, she'd rounded the potted plant and reached the table. The rose was there, but there was no man seated in the chair.

"I don't understand," Leslie said. "Do you think he saw me kissing you and left?" Leslie looked up into Tag's eyes. "I would hate to think I hurt that poor man."

"I can tell you with absolute certainty, you didn't."

Her brow furrowed. "Why? Did you tell him to leave?"

Tag shook his head, his lips twisting. "There's something else I needed to tell you."

Leslie tipped her head. "Is it about Joe?"

He nodded. "There never was a Joe Fox."

"You know who he was?" Leslie asked.

Again, Tag nodded.

"How do you know him?"

"I'm Joe Fox," Tag said. "I was your final match. I wanted you to get to know me without being biased by our friendship." He took her into his arms, a frown pulling his brow low on his forehead. "I hope you're not mad. I treasured our messages to each other. It helped me to see you from another angle as well."

She shook her head, her frown deepening. "You tricked me?" She pressed her hands against his chest. "Why would you do that?"

"I wanted you to fall in love with me. I thought we were too close as friends for that to happen. I wanted you to see me as someone who could be your friend and more." He tipped her chin. "But you fell in love with me as me. Not Joe. And that's even better." Tag kissed the tip of her nose, her cheek and finally her lips. "Please, don't be mad. I couldn't lose you. If you loved me as Joe, I would have changed my name to Joe Fox to make you happy."

Leslie stared up into his face. "I have to admit, Joe intrigued me. If I hadn't been so in love with you, I might have gone for him."

Tag sighed. "Sweetheart, you can have both of us. I've waited so long to say I love you, I can share you with my alter ego, gladly."

Leslie relaxed in his arms. "Why didn't you tell me sooner?"

"I wasn't sure that you loved me, and I couldn't declare my love and risk losing you as a friend. One way or another, you would always be a part of my life. I wanted you to love me, but I never wanted to lose you."

She cupped his cheek. "That's what I was afraid of, too. You've been such a big part of my life. I didn't want to risk losing you either."

He lifted the yellow rose from the table and handed it to her. "To new beginnings?"

"To new beginnings." She took the rose and smiled up into his eyes, her heart overflowing with emotion. "Can we go home now?"

"Aren't you hungry?" he asked.

"I have food in my refrigerator." She took his hand and led him toward the exit. "We can eat later. I've been dying to finish what we started the other night." She stopped and looked at him with narrowed eyes. "Why did you stop that night?"

"I didn't want to be a one-night stand. I wanted you to love me for me, not just for a quickie. And I didn't want you to regret it later."

"Darlin', you're not getting out of it tonight," she said. "I wouldn't have had any regrets that night. My only regret now is that we've wasted days we could have been together."

"I like the way you're thinking," Tag said. He gripped her hand and led her out of the restaurant. Soon, they were running for their vehicles.

"It's not a race," he warned her.

"The hell it's not," she said with a grin. Though she wanted to speed all the way home, she kept it barely above the posted limit, pulling into her driveway fifteen minutes later.

She had the door unlocked by the time Tag caught up with her.

Once they were through the door, he kicked it shut, yanked his shirt from the waistband of his trousers and grabbed the hem of her dress, pulling it up over her head and tossing it to the corner.

They left a trail of clothing from the front door to the bedroom, arriving at the bed naked and laughing.

When at last they fell into bed, they were wrapped in each other's arms, kissing like they had a lot of time to make up for.

Leslie knew tomorrow was never guaranteed. She wasn't going to waste another minute of happiness being alone. "I love you, Tag. Make love to me."

EPILOGUE

TAG AND LESLIE arrived at the restaurant together. They were done with all the trouble of arranging for separate dates. Instead, they'd asked Anne Blanchard and Milton Koch if they wouldn't mind going on a double date. Each had agreed.

"You think they'll mind us ditching them halfway through the meal?" Leslie said.

"I hope not," Tag said. "If they get along as well as Otis and Twyla—"

"And Herman and Chrissy—" Leslie added.

"Then they'll be planning their wedding before the main course is served," Tag said. He couldn't stop grinning.

"Are you worried they might be disappointed we aren't their dates?" Leslie asked.

"Not in the least. We're two for two, so far. I'm confident we're doing the right thing."

Leslie chuckled. "I think you like matchmaking even more than I do."

"I can't wait to see what BODS dreams up for Emma's brothers. I just know they're going to have the best matches. They'll all be married before the year is up."

Leslie's brow wrinkled. "I don't know. I think the system is a little glitchy. I might need to tweak it before the Jacobs brothers go out on their first dates."

"Oh, leave it and see what happens," Tag said. "What could possibly go wrong?"

"BODS could match them with people completely inappropriate for them," Leslie pointed out.

"Which might make it all the more interesting." Tag took her arm. "In the meantime, we have to match our dates. Then we can go home and start working on our own family planning."

"Family planning?" Leslie asked, cocking a brow.

"Well, yes. If we're going to have four children, we need to get going. If they turn out half as much fun as you, I might want to keep going until we have an even dozen." He winked and smacked her on the butt. His expression grew serious. "And, if you want, we can add Randy's kids to our bunch."

Her eyes widened and filled with tears. "Really? You'd do that for me?"

Tag cupped her cheek in his palm. "I'd do it for you and Randy. He was my friend. I know how much he wanted children. And having his child would keep Randy in our lives."

Leslie flung her arms around his waist and pressed her cheek to his chest. "I love you, Tag. More than you can imagine."

"I love you, too, sweetheart." He tipped her head up and pressed his lips to hers. Then he took her hand and walked her into the restaurant where Milton and Anne waited for them at the bar.

"I give them fifteen minutes," Tag whispered into Leslie's ear.

"Make it ten," Leslie said. "It might take a lot of practice to get our family plan started. We can't delay too long."

He grinned. "You're on."

THE BILLIONAIRE
GLITCH DATE

BILLIONAIRE ONLINE DATING SERVICE
BOOK #6

COMING SOON!

New York Times & USA Today
Bestselling Author

ELLE JAMES

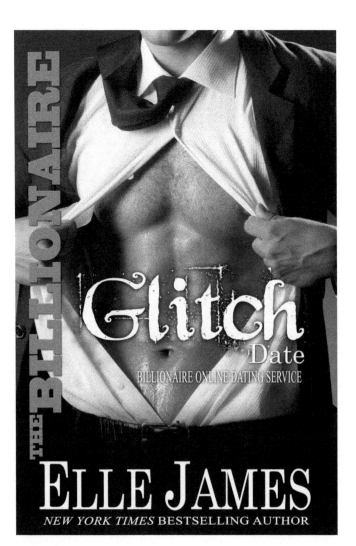

Glitch
Date
BILLIONAIRE ONLINE DATING SERVICE

ELLE JAMES
NEW YORK TIMES BESTSELLING AUTHOR

ABOUT THE BILLIONAIRE
GLITCH DATE

BILLIONAIRE ONLINE DATING SERVICE. Let us find your perfect match!

FINALLY CONVINCED to try the Billionaire Online Dating Service, Billionaire construction giant, Dillon Jacobs is ready to build his own home and wants to start the life of his dreams, with his perfect match. He likes control of his destiny and is looking for a woman who understands and fits in the tight little box of his world.

A former financial analyst, Ariana Davis learned you can't control everything. Her world crumbed around her when her fiancé died of cancer. To reground herself, she gave up her corporate job to make products to help people find the peace she so desperately desires. Though it's been years since her loss, she's not sure she's ready to launch into another relationship. When her friend from her grief counseling group convinces her to at least go out on a date, she agrees to just one.

A computer crash and a subsequent reboot creates a glitch in the system. Ariana and Dillon are matched but the jury is out on whether BODS got it right. Can two people who are so different possibly be right for each other?

PRE-ORDER HERE

DEJA VOODOO

CAJUN MAGIC MYSTERIES BOOK #3

New York Times & USA Today
Bestselling Author

ELLE JAMES

Careful what you wish for...

DEJA VOODOO

A CAJUN MAGIC MYSTERY

BAYOU MISTE

NAWLINS

Hotlanta

NEW YORK TIMES & USA TODAY BESTSELLING AUTHOR

ELLE JAMES

CHAPTER 1

BAYOU MISTE, LOUISIANA

"BOYETTE, I HOPE THIS IDEA WORKS." Edouard François Marceau scrunched his smartphone between his ear and shoulder as he sat on the bench by the back door of the rental cottage. With his hands free, he pulled off a muddy boot and dropped it to the porch planks. "If it doesn't, we may have us one dead witness on our hands, and that bastard Primeaux will get away with murder."

"Don't worry, it'll work," Ben Boyette, his partner in the Special Criminal Investigations Unit in Baton Rouge, reassured him. "Did you have any trouble finding the old trapper shack?"

"Did anyone ever tell you GPS devices work best on roadways, not waterways? Still, we managed with a few dead ends and switch-backs. If I lose this thing, I'll have to hire a tracking dog with gills to find them. Holy Jesus, that swamp is a freakin' maze! Marcus and I counted no less than nine alligators while we were out there. And those were the ones we could *see*."

"Did you point them out to our witness?"

"You bet." Ed shifted the phone to the other ear and attacked the laces on his left boot. "That ought to make even *her* stay put."

"You think? After the drug-running, backstabbing, mafia thugs she's been shacking up with, the alligators probably looked tame."

"Good point." One-handed, he tugged at the remaining muddy boot. The phone slipped, and he grabbed for it. "Tell me again why we're playing babysitter to a witness and why you didn't take this assignment?"

"Number one, I don't trust anyone else to get our witness to the courthouse alive. I suspect we have a mole in the force. And I'd have done it, but I'm up to my neck in trials over the serial rapist case." Ben sighed. "Since I did all the legwork, I'm the one in court. God, I hate courtrooms. But, we have to nail this guy so it sticks. Otherwise, I'd be there in a heartbeat. Oh, and I have a pregnant wife at home."

"Oh, yeah. That. Guess you're right. Although, I'd switch with you in a second. You're the one with all the experience wrestling alligators."

"You'll survive. Hopefully, the only alligator you have to wrestle is my moth—" Ben stopped in mid-sentence as if he changed his mind about what he was going to say next. "By the way, how are your digs? Mom buy your story?"

"Yeah." Ed padded through the small cottage, appreciating the homey feel of it. This was the kind of house he'd always pictured belonging to his grand-mother. If he'd ever known her. "I hate lying to your mom, though."

"She'll get over it. Did my share of fibbing to get out of doing the lawn a couple times growing up." He chuckled. "Come to think of it, I can still taste the soap. That woman could see right through every lie. She always caught me. But she loved me anyway."

"Yeah. She had to love you, you're her son." And Boyette was damned lucky to have her.

"I'm sure your mom did the same."

"Don't bet on it. Never knew her." His voice was a little harsher than he'd intended. A twinge of longing flickered across his subconscious, which he quickly squelched. No use pining after something he never had.

After all these years, he hadn't realized how much he missed having a mother until he'd met Ben's. Barbara Boyette was the consummate maternal figure. Care and concern written in every smile, wrinkle, and gray hair.

Ben cleared his throat. "Oh, by the way, do you like kids?"

Ed pushed his boots to the side and stood. Did he like kids? "Never thought about it. Why?"

"No reason. Did mom invite you to dinner already?" Ben asked.

"Nope."

Ben laughed. "Don't worry, she will."

"Is that bad?"

"Uh, no, not at all." Ben's answer was a little too swift for his comfort. "She moves quickly with single men."

"I'm not single, I'm divorced. There's a difference. Is there something you're not telling me?" He tamped down a sudden urge to get out of town. Fast.

"No, no. Nothing at all." Now Ben's voice sounded entirely too cheerful.

He should definitely run from this small town stuff as fast as his Nikes could take him.

"Mom's a great cook. She just sometimes cooks up more than her guests are ready to swallow."

Now he knew for sure Ben was keeping something from him. "What the hell do you mean by that?"

"Okay, so you're all set, then." Ben ignored his question. "Lay low and go fishing enough to keep Marcus and our girl fed and happy."

"Gotcha." He looked around the tiny cottage, the walls closing in on him already. "One question."

"What's that?"

"What the hell am I supposed to do with my time for the next few days?"

"Keep an eye open for suspicious characters. Otherwise, make like a vacation, and relax."

"I don't think I've ever taken a vacation." He scratched his head and thought back. No, he'd hung out at the office even on annual leave. All that use-or-lose vacation time got lost each year. "What do you do on a vacation?"

"Sleep until noon, girl-watch, you know, the usual thing."

"Maybe on Cocoa Beach, but in Bayou Miste? I'd go so far as to say the alligators outnumber the people. I don't think I've seen one live human besides your mother and the marina owner. Tell me, Ben, do they count the alligators in the census?"

Ben's outright laughter blasted Ed's ear. "Bayou Miste isn't that bad. Think about it, you arrived in the middle of the day, right?"

"Yeah. So?"

"School and work should be getting out by now." Ben chuckled again. "Just wait."

He didn't like the sound of his partner's laugh, it had a devilish quality. "Wait for what?"

"To meet the family. You're gonna love them."

"I thought it was just you and your mother."

Ben snorted. "Oh, no. I have eighteen brothers and sisters."

He fumbled the phone and almost dropped it. "Holy hell!"

"Yeah, that's what it's like around my house after school."

The introverted halls of Monti-Ed-zuma crashed around his ears.

Nineteen children in one family? What were his parents thinking? Obviously, they hadn't been thinking, they'd been—

"What have you gotten me into, Boyette?"

"You're a tough guy, you can handle it."

As the tune to "When the Saints Go Marching In" played on Alexandra Belle Boyette's phone for the sixth time in thirty minutes, she lay down on the couch and crammed a pillow over her ears. "Please leave me alone."

"Why don't you answer it and get it over with?" Calliope sat across from her, scraping the silver coating from a scratch-off lottery ticket, her long, wild, light red hair fanning across her shoulders like a cape. She wore a halter top and an ankle-length, tie-died peasant skirt, her legs tucked under her. No matter the circumstances, she always looked relaxed and carefree.

"No way." Alex sat up and leaned her face in her hands. "She'll ask me again if I've been seeing anyone, or she'll invite me to dinner at the house and drag some poor slob to the table with the family."

"So? What's wrong with that?"

"Even if I liked the guy, one look at my family and he'll run screaming into the bayou."

"Damn." Calliope frowned at the lottery ticket and tossed it onto the table. Then she looked across at Alex with a smile. "Your family's wonderful."

"Yeah, all nineteen of them." She rolled her eyes. "In this day and age, who in their right minds would have nineteen children?"

Calliope grinned "Your parents."

"Yeah, and what did it buy them?" She sat up. "An early grave for my father and insanity for my mother." Despite her flippant words, she still felt the pain of loss. Her father had been the rock in their lives and she missed him terribly, even two years after his passing.

"Alex, your mother loves every one of you and only wants to see you happy."

"I wish she could love me a little less."

"You don't mean that."

"Yes, I do. She won't leave me alone about love and relationships. I'm happy with the way things are. I have my own business, I'm in the best shape of my life. I have this great house. What more does she want?"

"Grandchildren?"

She snorted. "Big Brother Ben has that market

nailed. She'll have her first grandbaby in three months. Lucie's getting as big as the bayou."

"Speaking of Lucie, I saw her yesterday when I was in Baton Rouge. And you're right. She *is* getting big." Calliope smiled. "She looks great. Pregnancy must agree with her."

"Yeah, and Ben's over the moon. His chest is swelling so much, I doubt they can find shirts to fit him." Alex was happy for her brother. At the same time, a stab of intense longing hit her right in the gut. She had to suck in air to relieve the pressure.

"Oh, I almost forgot." Calliope jumped from her seat on the couch. "Lucie asked me to give you something."

She cringed. "Oh God, what now?"

Calliope fished in her pocket and dug out a small red velvet drawstring bag.

When Alex peered inside, she almost gagged. It smelled like something the cat dragged in from the swamp. "What is this stuff?"

"She didn't say. I bet five bucks it's some Voodoo remedy."

"Egad!" She dropped the bag on the end table. "You remember the last time she dabbled in Voodoo she almost had the entire town of Bayou Miste under her wacky love spell."

"But it all worked out in the end. Lucie married Ben, Maurice and DeeDee scheduled a Christmas wedding and Elaine and Craig eloped. The whole magic thing couldn't have turned out better. And, she's been taking lessons from her grandmother."

"Maybe that spell worked out all right, after a considerable amount of bad luck and a few murder attempts. But the one she put on Mo's pet alligator gave the poor beast a bad case of puppy love for Granny Saulnier's poodle. T-Rex still hasn't gotten over it."

"I don't know what it is. She asked me to give it to you the next time I saw you. I did and now my duty is done." Calliope blinked, all innocence. "Maybe it's a sachet you're supposed to put in your drawer to make your clothes smell good."

She wrinkled her nose "Not this stuff. It could make a grown man weep. I swear it has that rank odor of stump water." She shoved the bag toward her friend. "Take it back to her. I don't want to risk getting caught up in one of her crazy spells."

"Oh, no." Calliope held up her hands. "I'm not carrying that thing around. It might give me hair in places I have no business growing hair. Or worse, maybe it'll make me lose hair that I shouldn't. No, if you want her to have it back, you'll have to give it back yourself."

"Fine, I will. Next time I'm in Baton Rouge." She frowned at the sachet bag. "In the meantime, I have to put up with it. I hope it isn't anything dangerous."

The phone sang again and she flopped down on the couch pulling the pillow back over her head.

"Why couldn't I have had Lisa and Lucie's mother, who stays gone for twenty years at a time?"

Calliope stood at the sound of the third ring. "Because your mother loves you, and you should be nicer to her." She reached for the phone.

"Don't do it, Calliope," She warned. "If you value our friendship, you won't touch that phone."

Calliope cocked an eyebrow and punched the talk button. "Hello?" She listened. "Yes, Mrs. Boyette, Alex is right next to me. Sure. I'd be happy to relay the message. Seven o'clock? I'm sure that would be fine. Me, too? That would be nice. Good to talk to you, too, Mrs. Boyette. Bye, now."

"What did she want?"

"You and I are invited to dinner at her house at seven tomorrow night. Oh, and put on that slinky red dress you wore to Lucie's bachelorette party."

"My mother said that?"

"Well, most of it." Calliope grinned. "I added the part about the dress."

"Thanks, Calliope. Don't know what I'd do without you." She dripped sarcasm. "But I'm willing to try it."

Her friend dropped into the chair and tucked her legs underneath her. "I heard Lucie's Grand-mère LeBieu has been coaching her on Voodoo, again."

She punched her pillow and set it against the arm of the couch. "Should we consider moving to another state?"

The redhead tipped her head to the side as if considering her jest. "Possibly."

"Geesh. I just got the gym operating in the black, I hate to sell and start somewhere else."

Calliope's eyes lit up. "We could move to Biloxi."

With a very unladylike "Ha!" Alex stood and paced around the room. "That's the last place you need to move."

"Why?"

"Don't play dumb with me." She stopped in front of Calliope, planting her hands on her hips. "Biloxi would be entirely too much temptation for you. What, with a casino on every corner, it would be like navigating a minefield."

"I'm not that hooked on gambling. Besides, I could get a job in one of the casinos." Calliope's eyes twinkled and an excited grin spread across her face. "The pay and tips would beat what I get at the Raccoon Saloon."

"You should be happy you landed Lucie's old job. She got great tips."

"I guess moving is out of the question." Calliope's smile turned downward and she heaved a sigh. "I miss Lucie."

"Me, too," Alex said. "Why do things have to change?"

"Yeah," Calliope sighed again. "Why do people have to get married and move away?"

"Although, Lucie seems very happy." She could

still picture Lucie's glowing face at the wedding. How had she lucked into finding the love of her life here in Bayou Miste?

Calliope's eyes got all dreamy. "Do you think we'll ever find someone to love as much as Lucie loves Ben?"

"Not me. I only date the guys from hell."

"Like Theo?"

Alex rolled her eyes. "Why can't that bonehead take the hint?"

"Still botherin' you?"

As if to prove her point, her phone sang the theme for Jaws, the da dum, da dum sound grating on every last one of her nerves. She launched herself across the coffee table, snatched the phone, and cocked her arm to throw.

Calliope grabbed the device from her hand before she could let go. "Hey, don't ruin a perfectly good cell phone because of a guy."

She drew in a long breath and let out the tension with her exhale. "You're right. You're right. I'd miss my phone more than Theo."

"Not all guys are like Theo, you know," Calliope pointed out.

She snorted. "You haven't seen the ones my mom keeps throwing at me." She settled back on the couch and hugged a pillow to her chest. "I don't know where she gets them, but they've all had major 'me' hang-ups."

"What do you mean?"

"It's all about the guy." She wandered around her tastefully decorated living room where everything had a place and everything was in it. "Why can't I find a guy who thinks *I* hung the moon? A partner who will love me even when I'm majorly PMSing. Someone who will love me unconditionally, no matter how bad a day he's had."

As if he sensed how upset she was, Sport, Alex's golden retriever, trotted across the room and sat at her feet, his tail sweeping the floor in a steady rhythm. He stared up at her, mouth hanging open like he was smiling at her, his eyes pleading, "pet me".

She reached down and scratched behind his ears. "I don't think I'll ever find someone to love me like that."

"Sport loves you like that." Calliope giggled.

She laughed. "You know, Calliope, you're right. I need a guy like Sport. One who will greet me at the door, always happy to see me. Someone who can forgive me for forgetting his birthday. Someone who's happy no matter what I feed him or how fat I get." She squatted next to Sport and hugged him around his neck.

"Wouldn't it be neat if Sport were a man?"

"Yeah." She loved the silky feel of Sport's coat against her cheek. He loved her no matter what. "I wish he were a man. Then maybe my mother would quit trying to set me up."

"Hey, Sport." Calliope snapped her fingers. "Come here."

The dog laid a long wet tongue across Alex's cheek and wiggled loose to go to Calliope.

"How would you like to be a man?" The redhead rubbed her hand in his thick fur. "I bet you'd be really sexy, huh, boy?"

Alex stood and brushed the dog hair off her workout pants. "I have to get ready for work. Would you mind taking Sport out for a walk?"

"I'd love to." Calliope leaped from her chair. "Wanna go outside, boy?" She reached for the leash hanging on a hook inside the coat closet.

"Just don't let him whiz on Miz Mozelle's rose bushes. She never says anything, but I'm sure she doesn't appreciate it. I don't know what it is about her rose bushes that inspires him to grace them."

"We'll steer clear." Calliope snapped the lead on Sport's collar.

"And watch out for Granny Saulnier's poodle."

"FeFe?"

"Yeah. Sport has a thing for her. If you're not careful, he'll yank your arm out of its socket going after her."

"I'll be careful." Calliope paused with her hand on the front doorknob and looked back with her eyebrows raised. "Anything else before we go for a nice walk?"

"Get out of here." Alex lobbed a pillow at Calliope as she and Sport exited.

* * *

LATER THAT NIGHT, Alex lay in her bed, Lucie's Voodoo pouch lying on the pillow beside her. She'd had a particularly tough aerobics session at the gym and her muscles ached.

She lifted her cell phone and dialed.

"Hello?" Lucie's sleepy voice answered.

"Did I catch you doing something I only dream about?" she asked.

"Sleeping?"

"Never mind." She stroked the red velvet bag. "Is Ben home?"

"No, he's putting in a late day with the prosecuting attorney. You know, his criminal investigation stuff."

"What, and leaving his pregnant wife to fend for herself? Who's going to make the run to the convenience store for your latest cravings of sardines and pickles?"

"He's got orders to pick some up on the way home. How are you, Alex?"

"Great. I'm in the best shape I've been in a long time, I'm healthy, my business is booming and I've never been happier." Geez, she sounded like a broken record. A pathetic broken record, at that.

"Lonely, huh?"

That empty feeling gripped her belly and she automatically reached over the side of her bed to pat Sport's head. His wet nose nuzzled her hand. Was she lonely? Was that why she'd called Lucie in the first place? "Yeah, a little."

"Consider yourself hugged."

"Thanks." But a real hug would have been much warmer. From a real man—even better.

"Did Calliope give you the present?"

"Yeah. Actually, that's why I called." Alex lifted the pouch in her hand. "What is it?"

"A little Voodoo good luck for one of my best friends."

She grimaced. "Uh, gee thanks, Lucie. I can't tell you how happy it makes me."

"Relax, Alex." Lucie laughed into her ear. "You won't wake up as a frog or anything. My grandmother helped me with it, so don't worry."

"I can't tell you how relieved I am." Only slightly. Madame LeBieu knew her stuff. As the well-renowned Voodoo queen of the bayou, her spells always worked the way she intended. Unlike Lucie's.

"I can tell you're not thrilled." Lucie laughed. "Gran watched me every step of the way. She loves you like another granddaughter. Why would she propose something that would hurt you?"

"Let me remind you, she turned Craig Thibodeaux into a frog," she said, her voice flat.

"Yeah, but it all worked out in the end, didn't it?" Lucie sighed. "I love you, Alex. I just want you to be happy."

"I'm happy." Her hand tightened on the phone. "Why can't everyone figure that out?"

"Maybe you protest too much?"

"I'm not protesting." Alex realized, as she said it, she was doing just that. Her lips clamped shut.

"Is it a crime to want all my friends to be as happy as I am?" Lucie's voice drifted off.

She could imagine Lucie patting her swelling belly, and a sudden surge of maternal longing struck her right between the breasts. Why was she mooning over having a baby? Hell, she'd helped raise all her younger brothers and sisters. "I'm happy. Really." Even to her own ears, her voice wasn't very convincing.

"Give the Voodoo charm a chance, Alex. That's all I ask."

Lucie's voice cut through her ill temper and she relented. "Assuming I give it a chance, what is it supposed to do?"

A long pause met her question. Not a good sign. "I'm not exactly sure. Gran LeBieu said it would bring you good luck."

"In terms of what?" A chill swept down Alex's spine.

A whimpering sound rose from the floor beside her. Sport must have sensed her unease.

"It's okay, really. Gran LeBieu wouldn't give you anything that would hurt you."

"I'm shaking in my sheets here."

"Look, if you don't want it, bring it back with you the next time you're in Baton Rouge."

"I will."

"And when will that be?" Lucie demanded.

"As soon as I can break free from the gym." She knew that was an excuse. The thought of visiting Lucie in all her happy, pregnant glory made her own life look boring, lackluster, and downright sad.

"You're working too hard, Alex. Let Harry take over for a weekend. You need some down time."

She straightened her shoulders, refusing to give into downheartedness. "No, I like being busy."

"And you like going home alone?"

"Yes."

"Alex, it'll happen for you," Lucie said. "When you least expect it, love will knock you over."

"Like it happened with you?" She snorted. "I don't want to fall in love because of a Voodoo love potion. I want a man who loves me for me."

"Much as I'd like to take credit, my love spell never worked. Gran LeBieu confirmed, it had to be cast by a love bug, not a lady bug. If you remember, we couldn't find any love bugs, so we used a lady-bug. She let me think it worked to teach me a lesson."

"What?" She shook her head. "You mean my dumb

brother didn't need a kick in the pants to tell you he loved you?"

"Maybe he needed that kick in the pants, but he didn't need the love spell."

"I knew that," Alex said. She didn't know whether Lucie's news was good or bad. If the love spell didn't work, what were her chances at love? She fingered the velvet bag. "So, Lucie, what is this bag, really?"

"Gran LeBieu said it would help make your wishes come true."

Alex shuddered. "Kinda like my genie in a bottle?"

"I'm not entirely sure. I just thought you needed a little push, a boost to get you started."

"Look, Lucie, just because you're in love and that makes you happy, doesn't mean I have to be in love to be happy." But she had been pretty lonely since Lucie left. And she hadn't had a decent date in...When her visual memories started dating back to high school and she couldn't name a single unforgettable— happily they'd been forgettable—date, she grimaced. "Okay, I'll keep your gift for now, but I'm still not convinced I need it."

"Which makes me all the more convinced you do."

"I have my own business, my own home and a wonderful, if a little meddling, family. I don't need a love interest."

"Oh, Alex. You're my best friend in the world and I only wish you could feel how I feel."

"That's you, honey. And I'm happy for you." She

didn't add, and I miss you like crazy. Why mar Lucie's happiness?

"Oh, Ben just walked in," Lucie said. "Hey, *mon cher*, anything you want to say to your baby sister?"

The distinct sound of smacking noises carried across the line and Lucie giggled. "Beeennn, I'm on the phone with your sister." Another giggle.

A pang of longing twisted in her gut. Again. What the hell was going on?

"Alex? That you?" Ben's voice blasted into Alex's ear.

"Yeah, bro."

"Lucie's gotta go now."

More giggling erupted in the background and an indignant, "Ben! What about the baby?"

"Look, I have some ironing to do," she said. Suddenly, she couldn't stand listening to their playful antics on the phone.

"Yeah, okay," Ben said, obviously distracted.

"Tell Lucie I'll call tomorrow."

"Gotcha—damn..." A loud clunk was followed by dead air of being disconnected.

Alex plugged the phone into the charger on the nightstand and turned off the light.

She fought the strange pressure in her chest. What was wrong with her? She was happy. She sniffed. Was she coming down with a cold? Were her glands swelling in her throat, choking off her air?

A tear slid down her cheek. *Oh hell*. She didn't

need this. Self-pity was for weenies, not for black belts in karate or really kick-ass business owners.

She flung her hand out, bouncing it off the empty pillow beside her. The velvet pouch bumped against her fingers.

"Sport?"

After a brief pause, a cold, wet nose poked up over the side of the bed.

"I'm so lucky to have you." She ran her hand over his velvety snout. A long tongue snaked out and licked her fingers.

Sport was always there for her without being annoying or obsessive. Alex shivered. She'd had her share of boyfriends and stalkers. She'd rather remain celibate than go through that again.

But deep down, she ached for that closeness. And hell, she hadn't had sex in so long she wondered if she remembered how. Was she going to die one of those frigid old maids destined to read erotic romance novels to get her jollies?

I'm Pathetic.

And her mother would drive her stark-raving mad if she didn't quit shoving fresh meat at her every chance she got.

"Oh Sport, I wish you were a man. That would solve all my problems." She settled against her pillow and closed her eyes. "It would take a lot of magic to get my mother to back off. I'm not even sure having my own choice of a boyfriend will satisfy the woman." She yawned and snuggled in, pulling the comforter up to her chin to ward off the chill of the air conditioner.

As she drifted into a half-awake, half-asleep state, the bed sank down on the far side. Sport had leapt up beside her.

Too tired to tell him to get down, she gave up and let go.

A thrumming sound filled her dreams, building into a full bass echo of drums. Somewhere in the back of her sleep-numbed mind, she recognized the drums as those played at the Voodoo ceremonies Madame LeBieu conducted on those rare occasions when a little extra umph was needed to initiate one of her spells.

Just as she succumbed to oblivion, an eerie chant echoed through her head, "Wishes come true. Wishes come true. Wishes come true."

Alex sighed and gave in to the magic.

If only wishes really came true.

ABOUT THE AUTHOR

ELLE JAMES also writing as MYLA JACKSON is a *New York Times* and *USA Today* Bestselling author of books including cowboys, intrigues and paranormal adventures that keep her readers on the edges of their seats. When she's not at her computer, she's traveling, snow skiing, boating, or riding her ATV, dreaming up new stories. Learn more about Elle James at www.ellejames.com

Website | Facebook | Twitter | GoodReads | Newsletter | BookBub | Amazon

Or visit her alter ego Myla Jackson at mylajackson.com
Website | Facebook | Twitter | Newsletter

Follow Me!
www.ellejames.com
ellejames@ellejames.com

Hellfire Series

Voodoo for Two (#2)

Deja Voodoo (#3)

Cajun Magic Mysteries Books 1-3

SEAL Of My Own

Navy SEAL Survival

Navy SEAL Captive

Navy SEAL To Die For

Navy SEAL Six Pack

Devil's Shroud Series

Deadly Reckoning (#1)

Deadly Engagement (#2)

Deadly Liaisons (#3)

Deadly Allure (#4)

Deadly Obsession (#5)

Deadly Fall (#6)

Covert Cowboys Inc Series

Triggered (#1)

Taking Aim (#2)

Bodyguard Under Fire (#3)

Cowboy Resurrected (#4)

Navy SEAL Justice (#5)

Navy SEAL Newlywed (#6)

High Country Hideout (#7)

Clandestine Christmas (#8)

Thunder Horse Series

Hostage to Thunder Horse (#1)

Thunder Horse Heritage (#2)

Thunder Horse Redemption (#3)

Christmas at Thunder Horse Ranch (#4)

Demon Series

Hot Demon Nights (#1)

Demon's Embrace (#2)

Tempting the Demon (#3)

Lords of the Underworld

Witch's Initiation (#1)

Witch's Seduction (#2)

The Witch's Desire (#3)

Possessing the Witch (#4)

Stealth Operations Specialists (SOS)

Nick of Time

Alaskan Fantasy

Blown Away

Stranded

Feel the Heat

The Heart of a Cowboy

Protecting His Heroine

Warrior's Conquest

Rogues

Enslaved by the Viking Short Story

Conquests

Smokin' Hot Firemen

Love on the Rocks

Protecting the Colton Bride

Protecting the Colton Bride & Colton's Cowboy Code

Heir to Murder

Secret Service Rescue

High Octane Heroes

Haunted

Engaged with the Boss

Cowboy Brigade

Time Raiders: The Whisper

Bundle of Trouble

Killer Body

Operation XOXO

An Unexpected Clue

Baby Bling

Under Suspicion, With Child

Texas-Size Secrets

Cowboy Sanctuary

Lakota Baby

Dakota Meltdown

Beneath the Texas Moon

CPSIA information can be obtained
at www.ICGtesting.com
Printed in the USA
LVHW051548290420
654725LV00009B/791